An Actual Life

Also by Abigail Thomas

Getting Over Tom

An Actual Life

Abigail Thomas

Fic
Tho

Algonquin Books of Chapel Hill   1996

Published by
ALGONQUIN BOOKS OF CHAPEL HILL
Post Office Box 2225
Chapel Hill, North Carolina 27515-2225

a division of
WORKMAN PUBLISHING
708 Broadway
New York, New York 10003

LIBRARY OF CONGRESS CATALOGING-IN-PUBLICATION DATA
Thomas, Abigail.
    An actual life / Abigail Thomas.
      p.   cm.
    ISBN 1-56512-133-3
    1. Married people—New Jersey—Fiction.   2. Teenage mothers—New Jersey—Fiction.   I. Title.
PS3570.H5A88   9M
813'.54—dc20   95-40949
                                                           CIP
10 9 8 7 6 5 4 3 2 1
First Edition

For my family,
with love and thanks

An Actual Life

Part One

Would you have married me if I were a dwarf?" I asked Buddy to test his love.

"What?" He didn't look up from his book.

"Would you have married me if I were a dwarf."

"I doubt it."

"Why?"

"You wouldn't have looked the same."

This means he never loved me.

"How about if I were an albino?"

"Virginia, what's got into you?" Buddy turned around in his chair to look at me. His hair was messed up and he looked tired. "You know why I married you." At that exact moment the baby cried but then she went back to sleep.

"Dated me, then. Asked me out."

"No." Buddy shook his head. "I'm studying." He was sitting in my mother's old wing chair that she gave us when we got married. I was lying on the daybed with the green corduroy cover and the pillows that always slide off. Well, I had my answer.

Studying, I'm sure. He was probably writing Irene's name down fifty times in a row. It's something about her he just loves. I know it for a fact. And there's really nothing about me to love anyway. There's not even really any me, exactly. I keep changing inside my skin. There's no definite person in here. My voice comes out weird and I hardly ever say anything I mean.

We are going back to Hadley for the summer. We have to, it's Buddy's hometown. We were there last summer, too, before the baby came, when we first got married. I hate Hadley, I can't help it. The trees are short and the sky seems so much lower down than it does at home. I just feel all pressed in there, I don't know why. I also hate streets that are named after numbers. First Street, Second Street, how boring. Back home we name our streets for trees and flowers. I like Chestnut, and Elm, and Maple. Those are nice names for places to live. My old address is 39 Grove Street, Wellfleet, Massachusetts.

I look around before we leave but don't think I will miss this apartment. We only painted part of it blue. We ran out of steam in the living room where we only got the bottom half done. Above it is the pea soup color somebody else chose. I told Maddie the good thing about this summer is she can go right outside into her own yard but she's too small to know what I'm talking about. And it is the only good thing. Except of course for Dot. Nobody in Hadley can stand me except Dot. Everybody else thinks I am so stuck-up. Well, that shows what they know. A bunch of ignoramuses.

Aunt Dot has her camera ready when we pull into the driveway. Dot is who raised Buddy after his parents died. She and Buddy lived in this tiny white house and he loves her to death. "Cut it out, Dottie," said Buddy, giving her that really sweet smile that he has never once smiled at me. "Let me go, Dotdotdot," which is what he always calls her, after the punctuation. He unwraps her arms from around his neck. "Let me unpack the car," he says. But I can tell he was happy to see her. With Buddy you have to know how to read his movements because he seldom says anything affectionate in actual words. You have to see how he pretends to punch Dot's arm, or gets in his boxing crouch to pretend to box with her. This is Buddy's way of teasing and Dot just eats it up. I am more dignified, and my mother would just die if she could see this kind of behavior. I understand it somewhat, though. I wish he would do it with me once in a while. He never kids around with me in a friendly way. He says I have no sense of humor. Well, that is ridiculous. I have a very good sense of humor.

The house will be all for us this summer. Dot has moved in over the garage. "A little family needs its private moments," says Dot, with her Brownie snapping away pictures of us unloading the car. She gives me a big blue scrapbook for a present that she picked up at a garage sale and you can see glue from someone else's pictures on every page. I need something to keep my memories in, she tells me, and already I feel so bad. We aren't like that, Buddy and me, we don't have such sentimental feelings for our life. Dot holds me in her arms and gives me her skinny hard hug, then she holds me away from her. "Let me get a good look at you, Virginia," she says. "My, you do look beautiful. Isn't she beautiful, Buddy?" Buddy is on the spot and I feel almost sorry for him. He really doesn't like to make personal remarks. He just sort of grunts reluctantly uh-huh. "Now where's that little piece of sugar?" asks Dot, peeking in the window of the car where Maddie is still fast asleep in the backseat. I pick her up out of her seat and she is sweet and warm and heavy, and just waking up. Dot stretches out her arms and I put Maddie in them. At first I am worried that Maddie might not remember Dot, or be afraid of Dot, because actually Dot has a very small mustache but Maddie just snuggles into her arms and looks over at me with that funny little smile she gets. Dot is kissing and kissing away and stroking her hair and I wish I had put a little dress on Maddie instead of just her undershirt because this is sort of a special occasion. "Look at the curls on this child," exclaims Dot. "She's got your coloring, Virginia," she says. "And look at this fat little tummy!" tickling her and Maddie starts laughing. I love it when Maddie laughs. She sounds just like a mynah bird.

"How about a picture of this beautiful little family!" says Dot next. She always needs to be doing something. Dot does not just stand around all day. Buddy has a box of clothes under one arm and a suitcase under the other and he is pushing the car door closed with his foot. He is wearing his cowboy boots even though it is almost eighty degrees already. They make him six feet tall exactly. Otherwise he is five feet eleven although he always says six feet if somebody asks and he hates that I correct this every time. The last thing Buddy takes off every summer are his cowboy boots. I swear his feet must boil like soup in there but he doesn't care. They are some kind of lizard skin and have red decorations at the top and the toes are pointy. They look very uncomfortable to me. I tried on a pair at the store and I almost couldn't pull them off and I got sort of panicky. Buddy pulled them off for me, it was embarrassing because he had to put his foot against my chair and grab me around the heel of the boot and yank.

"Buddy, hold your daughter," says Dot, and Buddy rests the box on the hood of the car and puts the suitcase down and takes Madeline from Dot's arms. It always surprises me when Buddy does what Dot says. It feels funny standing there next to Buddy. This is closer than we usually stand and already I can feel the little part of Buddy that I do know getting farther and farther away. It is like his face is changing into a total stranger. Dot takes three pictures and lets us move around again. Buddy starts carrying things into the house. I am holding Madeline again and Dot and I are already laughing about Madeline trying to get down and play in the dirt. Buddy loved to play in the dirt, Dot tells me. I try to imagine Buddy as a baby boy but I can't.

The house is sweet. It has hollyhocks growing around the porch and the porch is only rotted out over in the front where nobody really sits. It has nice white posts and morning glories climbing up and the wicker rockers Dot drags out of the garage every spring and hoses down. Dot is still stringy as ever and today she has her hair in a tiny ratty little bun at the nape of her neck like Olive Oyl. Sometimes we have such a good time that I feel terrible. My mother is more restrained and she would be upset if she were a fly on the wall, so to speak, down here. She would not recognize me the way I am with Dot, how noisy I can be and how I laugh at ridiculous jokes my mother would never dream of making. My mother would not approve of all the dog hair in Dot's car or that her sandals are made of cheap white plastic. My mother believes in buying something of quality that will then last you a good long time. Dot has had her sandals for three years, though.

"Well!" I say, opening the screen door to the kitchen. "Here we are again!" I try to act as cheerful as I can.

Everything looks exactly the same. The same tablecloth with cactuses and the map of Colorado even though this is New Jersey. The same old bowl of plastic fruit in the middle of the table. Three fresh bananas on the counter. One black banana in a bowl by the stove for what purpose I do not want to know. The same old electric stove and the curtains with cherries and cherry stems over the sink. The same old yellowish sink. The same old ratty green rug by the door. The same old white paint kind of greasy over the stove. But it looks homey and Dot has pictures of Madeline on the fridge and even the smell of her cigarettes is kind of cozy and nice. I am sure if I look in the freezer I will find the piece of wedding cake I wrapped in tinfoil to eat on our first anniversary when I thought we were going to have a different kind of marriage. I bet it's still in there behind the old pork chops and the frozen spaghetti sauce and the exact same boxes of broccoli that were there last summer.

Sometimes I wonder if I will wind up in one small place most of my life the way Dot has. Already I have moved more times at age eighteen than Dot has in her whole life of forty-three. "Oh, you poor thing," she said when I first told her, "so many different schools?" but really I was thinking, Oh *you* poor thing you've always only lived in this sad tiny house that looks as if it might have blown down once and not gotten put all the way back up. This little house in this little place where all you can see is the black road and a few other houses along the way and across the street is a little brick building that has to do with the water supply and that has a chain-link fence around it and some weeds growing. It is kind of depressing. Our house in Wellfleet is larger and quite solid. We have a different kind of porch painted gray with a white railing and a lot more wicker furniture although the hollyhocks are spindly. My father is a minister and we have moved around the country a fair amount. I am not sure I could be happy staying put.

"How about some pop?" Dot asks, hauling bottles out of the fridge. "Anybody thirsty? Buddy? Virginia? How about you, little monkey?" she says to Maddie who is wiggling around in my arms. "Some pop for you?"

I have to say I hate the word "pop." I want to know what kind of drink it is. I want to know if it is Coca-Cola or root beer or a Dr Pepper. I don't like the word just "pop," as if it were all the same. I also hate, "Do you want some juice?" I want to know is it orange juice? Is it grapefruit juice? I think things should be named their own names specifically. Otherwise it is just lazy talk. That is how my mother feels about it and I feel exactly the same way.

"Pop-Pop!" Maddie is excited. She thinks it is her grandpa, who is my daddy, but we are not home at my house. This makes me feel so homesick for one minute, and guilty, too. I don't know what my daddy would make of my

life these days. I am afraid it would make him feel terrible.
I put Maddie in the old wooden high chair that used to be
Buddy's when he was a baby. Dot never throws anything
out. Maddie starts banging on the tray with her spoon and
yelling, "Like it, like it!" which she is smart enough to say
and not even quite one year old and I give her half a
banana. She wants one of the plastic ones so I have to pretend to be getting it from the bowl on the table. I peel it
for her and then she begins to mush it in her hands. I don't
really mind this, I think a child has to be allowed to make
some little messes. Then she throws it on the floor.

"Or iced tea? Would you like some nice iced tea?" asks
Dot, already mopping up the banana. I was going to do
that.

"Oh," I say to Dot, "I would love a glass of iced tea. It is
my favorite summertime drink. And a little apple juice
would be fine for Madeline. I'll get it, Dot, don't be silly,"
and I open the fridge again and get out the pitcher. She has
put the mint in as I feared. The mint grows wild around
the porch steps and the trouble is I have often seen dogs
pee there. I pour myself a very small glass with no mint in
it and then I take it into the bathroom and pour it down the
sink. I pretend I need a tissue for the baby. This is just the
beginning of things I can't eat here. "Delicious, Dot," I say.
I let Madeline have a small bit of apple juice in the plastic
cup. Buddy is marching in and out of the kitchen with the

suitcases and boxes like a one-man procession of ants. I love the sound the screen door makes banging behind him. I don't know why. I wish Buddy would smile sometimes. But he isn't that kind of person and there's nothing I can do about it.

We are going to be sleeping in Buddy's old room with the twin beds which Dot has pushed together. This makes me so sad for Dot. She doesn't know we don't care at all if our beds are touching since we don't really lie down in bed and do anything together. Actually, I'm just as glad if you want to know the truth. The first thing I want to do is screech them apart but I can't do that except very gradually, like an inch at a time. The wallpaper is brownish with some green leaves thrown in and it is peeling by the window. The plaster is furry underneath where there was an old leak. The window is high in the wall, and there is only one in the whole room. "Good room for a baby," says Dot, "nice and dark," which I do not think is true. My baby prefers a little sunlight for her naps. Buddy's old high school pennants are on the wall and Maddie's crib is going right underneath them. Buddy's going to put it together when we're done unpacking.

Dot is fussing away helping me put our things in the drawers. She has a special pink dress for the baby that she picked up at the flea market. "Oh, Dot," I say, "this is awfully nice," although I don't actually think so since it is covered with lacy frills. It will make Maddie look like a little store-bought cake. My tastes are much simpler, as are my mother's. But it is so easy to make Dot happy. You just act happy around her and thank her for everything she does. I sometimes feel disloyal to my mother when Dot and I are laughing. It is hard to say what we find so funny, but in certain moods it is almost everything.

"I saw this sign, Dot," I say to her. She is folding up Maddie's undershirts and putting them in the top drawer. "It said HOUSE FOR SALE. But the H was painted funny and it looked like MOUSE FOR SALE. Isn't that funny?" Dot thinks it's funny too, thank goodness. She says, "Mouse for sale? Oh! Mouse for sale! Oh!" and then she starts laughing this terribly loud laugh that would drive my mother crazy but usually sends this surge of happiness into me. One time Dot nearly drove her car off the road from laughing so hard. "Oh dear!" says Dot. "Oh dear! I wonder what they were asking for it!" she says, which starts me off laughing again.

"Well, if it was a very special mouse it might be worth five dollars," I say. It is all so silly but that's what we laugh at, me and Dot.

"What's up?" Buddy asks. He is dropping the last box down on the bed. He acts like there might be something wrong with us laughing this hard. Maybe he thinks we're laughing at him. "Mouse for sale," I tell him. "Remember?"

"Oh," says Buddy.

Dot and Maddie and I go sit outside on the porch while Buddy puts the crib together. He can do anything mechanical. It is so different from my daddy who can't even bang a nail in the wall, or so my mother says. She is proud of that fact, however.

The old beat-up dog that wandered into Dot's yard last summer I am sorry to say is still around. She named him Old Dog because that's what he certainly is. Gray around the everything. "Hello, Old Dog," I say, but I don't care to see him sitting right on the porch however, licking himself and then that awful thing just comes poking out like a big red lipstick. "Shoo!" I say to him when Dot goes inside for a minute and I'm just out here with Maddie in my lap. "Shoo! You horrible old thing!" Thank God nobody hears me. I don't care if he is old. He is also horrible. On top of that I know that dogs can read your mind and see right through you. Old Dog must know that I can't stand him. They can tell from your tone of voice, and from the way you smell, too.

"Where's Buddy?" I call into the kitchen to Dot after a few minutes.

"On the phone in the hall calling Chick," says Dot. "How about a bite to eat?" she asks, as if there were nothing wrong. "Tuna okay?" She pokes her face outside the screen door. "You want chips with it?" She is wearing the red and white checked apron I gave her for Christmas. It says KISS THE COOK on the front. She is too happy to notice anything wrong with me. And she doesn't have such a suspicious mind.

"I'll just have tomatoes, if you don't mind," I say, but I feel so terrible. Chick is Buddy's oldest friend but he is also married to Irene. This is the part I hate and it has already started. Here Dot is acting like we're the cutest happiest little family in the universe and Buddy is calling up Irene. I saw the old green pickup in her driveway which is down the street from here I am sorry to say. I saw him see it too, and watched him look at it in his sideview and then his rearview mirror as we drove past. He does not know I was watching but I was.

Dot comes outside and takes Madeline down to the garden and I go into the kitchen and bang things down on the table hard. *Bang* goes the thermos bottle which I hope I break. *Bang* goes a can of peaches. I can hear Buddy talking to her. "Hey, Irene," he says, in that soft voice he never uses when he speaks to me. "Yeah. Today. Yeah. All summer. Sure thing, yeah." He hangs up the phone but doesn't move. He stays in the hall.

"Ahem," I say, but he still doesn't move. "Who was that?"

"What? Oh, that was Irene." As if he is telling me the weather.

"What were all those yeahs about?" I ask in my iciest

voice. Dot is outside picking tomatoes for lunch with the baby and I feel I can speak freely.

"Oh, she asked after the baby."

"And the baby was yeah?"

"She asked if the baby was fine. She asked if you were fine. I said yeah. Is that a crime, Virginia? Are you going to start that all over again?"

"Are *you* going to start this all over again is more like it," I say.

He just keeps his back to me.

This is what worries me. It must be true love if he loves her and she is not even pretty.

It is bad luck to stir with a knife and a minute later Buddy uses one to mix the sugar in his coffee and I let him. I don't remind him. I knock on wood while he's doing it though, just to keep the bad luck down to a minimum. It feels too funny just to let him expose himself that way to the forces of nature. At least, I have told him time and time again, at least use the handle not the blade. But Buddy pays no attention to any of this. He thinks I am ridiculous. Well, I hope I do not have the last laugh is all I can say.

I love you," I said to Buddy over and over the spring before last. We were in his dorm room with the door closed and we'd hooked a chair under the knob so nobody could come in. It was just a little bedroom with a really high ceiling but otherwise it was like a cell, really. Buddy rolled off me and he snapped on the light.

"What's wrong?" I asked. "What's the matter?" I was so nervous. I was afraid he would see my bra with all the safety pins and gray elastic. I usually took my own bra off first and stuffed it into my bag. My underwear isn't always in the best of shape. But tonight had just happened so fast I didn't get the chance and now Buddy was staring at the sheets. "Move over," he said. I wrapped the blanket around me since I am actually very modest and leaned against the wall. "What are you doing?" I asked him. "What are you looking for?" I hoped he would never see my underpants which were in a corner of the room. God.

"Blood," he said. "There's supposed to be blood." He was whipping back the top sheet all the way to the foot of the bed.

"Oh, that's right," I said. "I know. Do you see any?"

Buddy shook his head. Finally I found a speck of red underneath where I had been lying. "Here it is," I said, but I could tell Buddy was disappointed. Maybe he didn't even believe it was my first time. But it was. Swear to God, it was. I can't help it if I didn't bleed. It didn't even hurt. But there I was, with a bun in the oven that very night for God sakes. It was so easy.

ℒast night there was a cricket in the living room and I couldn't sleep. I had to wake Buddy because I was scared to go to the bathroom. The crickets here are as big as little mice. I woke him as nicely as I could.

"Buddy?"

"Mmmmm."

"Buddy, wake up." I shook him. "Buddy, there's a cricket." I whispered it loudly in his ear.

"What?" But he wasn't really paying attention. I pinched his arm just a little.

"Buddy, there's a cricket in the living room I think and another one in the bathroom over by the toilet. I can hear them."

"Why are you telling me this, Virginia? It's two A.M." He held his arm over his eyes.

"Because I have to get up."

"So get up." He turned back to sleep again.

"I can't, Buddy. There's a cricket. I told you."

"What do you want me to do about it?" He propped himself up on one elbow and his breath smelled sour but I suddenly really wished he'd kiss me. But of course he didn't.

"I want you to wrap it up in tissue paper and drop it out the back door. Both of them."

"You do?"

"I don't want you to kill it. Them."

"You don't?"

"No. It's very bad luck to kill a cricket especially when it's in your house." I said this even though I was afraid he'd get up and smash the poor cricket with his shoe but he surprised me. He caught them both and put them both out back. I heard the screen door bang and then he came back to bed.

"Are you happy now, Virginia?" he asked. I got up to pee. "Thank you very much," I said, the bed creaking. "Don't mention it," said Buddy. I tiptoed down the hall and stood there quietly listening but all the crickets were outside the house. It sounded like all the crickets in the world. When I got back in bed Buddy was snoring away and I very lightly put my arm around his shoulders and fell asleep myself. In the morning I woke up the way I always wake up, way over on my own little bed with the pillow over my head and Buddy already in the shower.

My mother calls and Buddy answers the phone. He has not always got the most perfect manners. "Hi, I'll get Virginia," is all he says to her. He puts the phone down on the table and bawls out my name. "Virginia! Telephone!" He doesn't even say, "Virginia! Your mother is on the phone!" I know my mother will be galled by this because it is like ignoring her. But Buddy doesn't know what to say to her. He knows what to say to Dot. "Hey, Dottie," he says, "howzit goin'?" If he said "howzit goin'" to my mother she wouldn't know what to say.

"Mother," I say to her now, "how are you and Daddy?"

"Your father is fine, Virginia." She has an icy tone in her voice.

"How about you? How are you?" Sometimes you have to coax her to talk about herself even when you know that's why she called.

"Oh, I'm fine, Virginia," she says, but I can tell she is furious about something. It always makes me nervous until I find out what it is. Like anything I say might be the trap door that I'll fall through. You never can tell what will tick my mother off.

"Well, that's good," I say. I don't know what else to say. There is a horrible pause.

"Mrs. Mercher says Elinor had a letter from you." She says the word "letter" as if it were a spider.

"I sent Elinor a letter," I say as brightly as possible considering the froggy guilt I can feel in my throat. I don't even know what I've done yet. What did I say in the letter that could make my mother so mad?

"I understand you sent several photographs." My mother's voice has that sound you make by rubbing a balloon with your hands. I don't know how she does it. I have tried but I can't make my voice do that. Nobody pays any attention. Buddy just looks at me and laughs.

"Yes, I did," I say, trying to sound cheerful. I sent Elinor a couple of pictures of me in my wedding dress after I spilled grape juice down the front. I forget what I wrote. It was after Buddy and I had gone back to our new apartment at school. Ages ago.

"I understand something spilled on your new dress." She means wedding dress but she won't call it that. Nothing about the wedding made my mother happy but she got through it anyway.

"Oh," I say, "it was terrible. But I didn't ruin it, Mother," I say. "I soaked it after." A big fat lie. I threw it out.

"It looked ruined to me. I gather you found it all rather funny, too. I'm just surprised at you, that's all, Virginia. I thought you quite liked that dress."

That's how she gets sometimes. "Oh, Mother, I loved the dress! Really!" You can go on and on like that but she gets it in her head a different way and it hurts her feelings. When you hurt her feelings she gets pretty mad. The thing is, I hated the dress. It had ruffles on the front and it was puffy-sleeved and it made me look like I had stuffed some mashed potatoes down my front instead of having a nice figure. I didn't like it at all, and I was glad that I stained it so bad. It was kind of a gray color. "You certainly cannot wear white," my mother had said.

I don't know why this made her so mad. Probably she thought Mrs. Mercher was talking behind her back. My mother does not like to think people might talk about her or know something she doesn't know, or anything like that.

She does not like that I might not have appeared proper in that picture or whatever I wrote to Elinor which now I can't remember. It's Mrs. Mercher's fault partly too, to go snooping around in Elinor's things. I'm sure Elinor wouldn't have told.

"Elinor Mercher is getting married," my mother tells me now. "He is some sort of royalty. I believe they will settle in Bologna." She pronounces it the Italian way.

"Oh, that's great," I say, imagining my voice like this flat tire I need to jack up. This is one of her ways of being mad at me for what happened, for having to get married. She is saying look what you threw away. A proper marriage. "Kings adored you, Virginia," she said to me once, after she had been crying a long time. That is because once in Switzerland a tiny little midget asked me out and he happened also to be heir to the throne of the smallest kingdom in the world. This is actual fact. Except he asked everybody out. I have told my mother this. She refuses to pay any attention. In her mind if a king asked you out that's all that mattered. You had a shot at something really big. It is very embarrassing to hear her talk about this. He didn't love me and he wasn't a king. He was some sort of tiny prince. But even if he had been I wouldn't have gone out with him. Once I saw him picking his nose. I didn't wait to see what he did with it after he looked at it on the end of his finger. I was afraid he was going to eat it. I just went back to my game of checkers and pulled my hat over my face.

To cheer Mother up I tell her that Maddie is not too happy here. "She keeps saying your name," I tell her. This is actually a lie but it makes my mother sound happier. "Well, that's very nice, Virginia," she says. Actually, Maddie loves Dot and the only name she really says is Pop-Pop.

We haven't been here three days and suddenly Buddy decides he wants a tattoo. What's going on? Why would you want to do that when you're already married to someone? He gets all offended when I ask him. "Can't I do anything around here without getting the third degree?" says Buddy. Well, if he asks me why I'm wearing my red sweater when I'm already married to him I don't see why I can't ask why he wants a tattoo for God sakes. "Who do you expect to impress, Buddy Wilcox?" I ask with my hands on my hips. It just does not seem right that he should be able to go sauntering all over town like a damn sailor when I'm stuck at home with the baby. Fortunately Maddie is already asleep. I don't believe in arguing in front of a child. And Dot has gone to bed early too.

Buddy doesn't pay any attention. He is too busy marking a place on his arm where he wants to put it. He has a blue pen and he wants me to draw his initials right on the side of his muscle. Then I am sure he will want me to poke holes in his skin. How can he think I would do such a thing? "If you don't want to do it I'll find somebody else," he says, and I hate him in this instant. I know who he is talking about. Irene. I know for a fact that Buddy and Irene went out all through high school. I happen to have his yearbook. There are a million pictures of Irene sitting on Buddy's lap for instance, with her skirts hiked up, which I can't imagine how they printed it in a school publication. She is always in the picture with Buddy except when they were photographed on their horrible sports teams. It makes me sick to look at these pictures because I get so upset and jealous. And this is what is written under Irene's picture in Buddy's yearbook. "Hey, Buddy-boy, hang on to it for me next year, willya?" and then a heart with her initials and his inside, and then "Your Irene." It makes me sick to read that. First, it is disgusting. Hang on to it for me, willya? I hate that. I hate the "willya" and I despise what she is probably talking about. Every time I think about it I just want to faint or die. And I can't stop looking at it, either. Even though it makes me sick.

Buddy is staring into the mirror in the bathroom with his hair brushed back like a damn movie star and the ballpoint in his hand. He has just woken up from a nap, too, and his cheek is all indented with the pattern of the bedspread. I used to feel so funny when he had just woken up like that, like a child, it made me want to hug him. But you can't do that with Buddy. It is like hugging this dangerous tuning fork. You can feel him thrumming and he doesn't put his arms around you back. It can be very embarrassing so I never do it anymore.

"How are you going to find a job with a tattoo?" I say, which is ridiculous, since Buddy already has a job and he has already started work painting houses. He ignores me, of course. "And exactly what is this tattoo going to be?" I ask.

"My initials," says Buddy. "B. W."

Well, that's better than a skull and crossbones. "Don't you want to put a heart around them?" I ask, hoping he will decide to put my initials next to his initials inside the heart. I could never suggest such a thing outright. It would be too embarrassing. But he doesn't even seem to have heard that.

"Get a needle, will you, Virginia?" he says. Well, I pretend we don't have any needles.

"All we have is a pin," I say sweetly. "Will that do?"

Buddy nods. "Anything to make the holes so you can put the ink in." He holds up a bottle of Quink.

"We'll need ice to freeze up your arm so it won't hurt too much." I can't believe I'm saying this. The last thing I imagined was that I'd ever be sticking pins in Buddy's skin.

"Ice it is, then." And he actually smiles at me. "Thanks, Virginia," he says. God. The vision speaks. He goes into the kitchen and I can hear him breaking out the ice tray and several cubes hit the floor and skitter. Buddy swears but he sounds happy. He is probably excited to think how sexy he is going to look swaggering around Hadley.

I quickly put a couple of Chiclets in my mouth since my face is going to be right next to his face in order to draw on his arm. This is the closest we have been in months without having a baby to pass back and forth. His breath is somewhat garlicky from the take-out Chinese food last night but I don't really mind it when Buddy's breath smells bad. I don't know why, it just doesn't bother me. We get ready, I turn on the big lamp and tell him to sit right underneath and he does. I start to write his initials. "Did you ever hear about lockjaw from an infected tattoo?" I ask him in a sweet tone of voice. "Or hepatitis?"

Buddy shakes his head. "Nope."

"Well, there's this terrible disease where they have to break your jaw in order to get it open again. It comes from skin infections from getting a tattoo." I keep tracing away. "Did you ever think of maybe just growing a mustache instead?"

"Stop trying to talk me out of it."

"I'm not trying to talk you out of it. I'm just asking you if you know what can happen. And I think you would look extremely good in a mustache. At least you wouldn't have to turn yellow and have your jaw broken open with a little hammer." I'm done writing his initials and I hold the ice on his arm now. "This should freeze up in just a minute," I say, as if I know what I'm talking about. "Have you had a tetanus shot in the last four years?"

"You don't get tetanus from a straight pin, Virginia."

So then I give his arm a pinch. "You better have something to bite down on," I say, and give him the July *Ladies' Home Journal*.

"Have you done this before?" Buddy sounds nervous now, but it's too late. He asked for it. He closes his eyes. You'd think I was using a damn sword.

It's amazing how difficult it is to stick a pin through somebody's skin even if you think you don't care how much it hurts them. I feel sort of sorry for him, and I can't stick the pin in as hard as I should the first time and it doesn't puncture his skin. On top of that my fingers are slippery and the pin is painful to push down on. "Is it in yet?" he asks, taking the magazine out of his mouth. "Not quite, just hold still, Buddy." He holds still. I try again. "Is the ice wearing off?" I ask him. "Jesus Christ, Virginia," he says, with his eyes squeezed shut, "how hard can this be?" which of course makes me mad. "I can't help it if you have really thick skin, Buddy," I say, "and on top of that I don't think you realize how slippery this pin is. I really need a thimble, if you want to know." My fingers are brushing his arm the whole time and I know my hair is tickling his face. He has to keep blinking. He probably can't stand being this close to me for so many minutes. "Just stick it through, Virginia," says Buddy. "Come on. How hard can this be? Jesus." So I stick it in as hard as I can, and he yelps and hops off the chair. "Forget it," he says. "Just forget it."

Old Dog wanted the ice so bad but I gave him a piece of melon instead. It turns out Old Dog is a sucker for melon of any kind. I just scooped out a nice ball of it and rolled it across the porch to him. He was so pathetically happy he didn't even realize I should have brought it to him, not rolled it. *Thump* goes his tail on the floor. *Thump thump*.

Then we went to bed, or rather Buddy went to bed. I sat up on the living room couch for a while because I wasn't sleepy and if there's one thing I hate it's lying next to Buddy in bed wide awake while he's snoring away to beat the band, probably having one good dream after another, and I'm wondering, What am I doing here?

Old Dog comes and scratches on the screen. I feel sorry for the horrible old thing so I let him come in and his toenails click across the floor and first he sniffs around and then he comes over and clumps down next to me and I have to pet him even though he is horrible to look at and also I am sorry to say he is horrible to smell. Old Dog has digestive difficulties and my eyes water from the terrible smell he makes right next to the sofa. "That's quite enough, Old Dog," I say, standing up, and the magazine falls right off my lap. But he looks up at me with those sad

old eyes and his tail thumps on the floor and I can't put him
out. Instead I get my trusty can of Pledge and spray the air
a little and that makes it some better. I don't know why
Old Dog likes me. I thought dogs could read your mind.
But this one seems not to know that I find him revolting.
Although there is something very nice about an old animal
who you don't know from Adam who comes and sits next
to you for no reason just to keep you company and lays his
chin across your foot.

Maddie and I go down to watch Buddy play ball. It's Saturday, his only day off practically. I walk the back way so I
won't run into anyone on the street. Maddie hates her
stroller so I'm pushing the stroller and carrying her, which
is no doubt a ridiculous sight but I can't help that. The ball-
field is behind the school. I can see Buddy out in the field;
it is easy to make him out because his T-shirt is bright
orange and his hair is so black. I wish it didn't give my
heart always a lurch when I see him like that from a distance. I wish I didn't care how handsome he is, because I
don't, actually, when you get right down to it. So what if
he is handsome. He has never once said, "Virginia, you are
my one true love. I love you and only you." This is because
I am not. Irene is, I'm sure. I have seen him look at her
with that frozen electrical look on his face. There is
nothing wrong with Irene. It doesn't matter that she is cov-

ered with makeup and wears an ankle bracelet. I just don't
know what he sees in her and it scares me. "Look, Maddie!
There's your daddy!" and I start shouting Buddy's name.

Of course he acts like he doesn't recognize me, as if he
can't quite remember who I am. "Ohhh," he says, like he
can barely make me out, squinting like I'm a speck in the
distance although I am practically standing on his toes with
Maddie bawling her head off right in front of him. "Ohhh,
it's you, Virginia."

Well, who else would it be? Who else would be holding
his sopping wet baby?

"Go on home," he says. He doesn't even like me to come
and watch. He plays third base and I like to look at him out
there and pretend that he is pretending not to see me
because of how much he loves me and how it might throw
his whole game off. How he has to keep from running out
of the game to embrace me and Maddie and introduce us
all to his teammates as the secret of his success. Of course
this is just what I have in my mind as a wish. He certainly
never would do such a thing. "Go on home," is what he
really says after I have waved at him like bloody murder to
get him to come over. "It's too hot here for the baby." He
keeps looking back at the team to see if they are staring.
There are lots of other people watching the game but
mostly they are girlfriends and nobody else has a baby
except me. Everybody is looking but I don't care and I

don't care if I raise my voice a little. "Why not?" I say loudly. "Why shouldn't I come down here? What's the matter?" Buddy just pats my arm.

"For the baby's sake," he says, using his snow-job voice. "She'll get a burn."

"I have brought a hat for her," I say, pulling it out of my pocket, "and I have put tons of suntan lotion all over her. Here. Smell." And I hold up Maddie's little arm to his face. Meanwhile of course all Maddie wants to do is get down and eat dirt. I know her. She's wiggling and squealing and trying to get down on the ground.

"It's ninety-three," says Buddy. "She'll get heatstroke. She'll get a burn." And he takes her wriggling out of my arms and lifts up her shirt and smooches her tummy and hands her back for which I cannot say thank you since it has only made matters worse and now she is yelling. Maddie has a very loud yell. This is getting embarrassing. "Go on home," says Buddy, giving me a little push, but nicely. "I'll be back right after the game." Maddie is trying to grab him now, and she is like holding a great big wiggling trout. She is wearing only an undershirt and a pair of diapers and everything is starting to fall apart. One of her red socks is kicked off and I don't even know where it is.

"Well, how long will that take?" I keep asking. "How many innings? Do you promise?"

"Cross my heart," says Buddy and I watch him run back

onto the field. So I pick up the bag with all Maddie's things
in it, her nice cold bottle and a couple of diapers, and I walk
back across the street. Next thing I know, I'm walking down
Fourteenth Street and there is Irene slowing down in her
green truck. She stops and pokes her head out the window.

"Hey," she says, "I thought it was you," and she smiles at
me in a friendly way. My heart is pounding. I didn't expect
to see Irene. I can see little trickles of perspiration running
down her cheeks. Her skin is pale and her hair is so pale
and thin. Even all sprayed up it's starting to melt on her
head. I want to wipe her face with one of my extra diapers
because it gets to be your instinct to mop up when you are
a mother. She is wearing bright blue eyeliner on her lower
eyelids which makes her look like a poisonous lizard.
"How's it going?" she asks.

"Oh, just fine," I say, imagining a lizard tongue darting
out of her mouth, "although it's a little hot for the baby," and
I transfer Maddie from my right hip to my left. By now
we're just slippery with sweat, both of us. I don't know why
I even bother to bring the stroller since Maddie hates it.

"Get in," she says, and it's really like an order. "It's too
hot to walk." So I do. There isn't much time for chitchat
since it's only a few blocks to the house. Her truck is clean
as a whistle except for a can of Dr Pepper rolling on the
floor, and she has a Saint Christopher medal hanging off
the rearview mirror. Irene always has a can of Dr Pepper in

one hand. She pulls into our driveway to let us out. "Babies get hotter than toast," she says, looking at us, and she leans close to Maddie's face and blows very gently on the top of her head. Maddie stops wriggling. Irene doesn't say anything like Oh how adorable she is, she just blows on her head again very softly. This is no doubt because she has had her fill of babies with all the little brothers and sisters. "What's wrong with Buddy that he keeps you to himself so much?" she asks, looking at me with those weird eyes. I want to say he isn't keeping me for himself, he just doesn't want me around anywhere he is.

"I think he's just embarrassed," I say, although I don't know why I should be confiding in Irene of all people.

"Well," says Irene, "I think he should be proud of his little family. And I'd be happy to tell him so. Maybe Buddy should learn to own up to his responsibilities."

"Oh, he does," I add quickly. "He works all the time, all the whole time."

Irene is letting Maddie play with her sunglasses now, Maddie is mashing them down on her head. "How about you guys come over for supper one night?" she asks.

"Oh, that sounds very nice," I say. "But I'll have to check with Buddy. He is very busy this summer. Look out now, Madeline, you don't want to break the nice lady's glasses," and I get them out of her little fists somehow and hand them back to Irene. "Thank you very much for the ride," I say loudly, over Maddie's noisy protests. She wants the glasses back. "Like it, like it!" Maddie keeps yelling.

"Sure thing," says Irene. "You be good now," she says to Madeline, who has started crying and poking her finger in her little nose.

"She's tired," I say. "She isn't usually so crabby," I say because by now Maddie is screaming and it is kind of embarrassing. "You must have had enough of babies," I say climbing down from the truck.

"What?"

"Well, I know you come from a big family." I wish I hadn't gotten into this. Irene's mother had to clean banks at night because their father ran away and Irene had to make supper for everybody and pack all their lunches and change all their diapers et cetera. I know this from Dot although Dot doesn't usually talk about Irene.

"Well," says Irene, "you get used to what you have to get used to." And she smiles. "Let me know if you need a lift anywhere else," she says, backing the truck down the driveway. I can't help thinking Irene is very nice.

"Okay," I yell back, although that is out of the question. Maddie and I stand there waving for a minute and Irene beeps her horn.

I am just grateful she didn't tell me anything about Buddy like what a hard worker he always was as I do not care to hear about Buddy from the lips of his old girlfriend but all she said was she would be calling in a few days and maybe we'd all barbecue together sometime. I feel much better after seeing Irene. She doesn't seem interested in Buddy, at least not in that way. And she has her own problems.

"Was that Irene's truck I saw?" asks Dot. She is drying the dishes when I get in. It is like Dot to come over and do my work for me. "Yes, it was, she was nice enough to give us a ride."

"Mmmhmm," says Dot. I cannot explain what kind of sound Dot makes but it is not friendly toward Irene.

"What?" I ask. "What do you mean?" Dot and I can talk this kind of shorthand.

"Oh, I don't know," says Dot. "I just couldn't be too careful around that one." But she won't say any more. For some reason Dot does not like Irene. I think it's because she is on my side. Dot is very protective of Buddy if she thinks someone is after him. I heard her shaft all kinds of girls last summer who hadn't heard Buddy was married.

And when does he come home? Twelve o'clock midnight, thank you very much. And when I yell at him what does he do? He laughs and he burps. He burps and he thinks it is the funniest thing he ever heard in his life. But he slept on the sofa thank God. I didn't want to be in the same room with him. I'd rather sleep with Old Dog farting under the covers than sleep with Buddy when he's in that condition.

Every morning when Maddie wakes up I take her in bed with me in hopes that she will fall back asleep for a little while but she sits on my chest and talks to me excitedly. "Mama!" says Maddie. "Up! Up!" and she tries to open my eyes with her fingers, which always makes me laugh. So I get up and we go in the kitchen and drink orange juice and she has a banana and I drink three cups of coffee. The first cup has cream and sugar and the next two cups are black as I am training myself to drink my coffee black as my parents do. Then we feed Old Dog out on the porch if Buddy hasn't already done that and then we sit in the backyard. Sometimes we don't even get dressed first. Nobody comes back here so it doesn't matter if I'm still in my bathrobe and Maddie is just in her diaper. I love to watch Maddie play. Maddie doesn't sit on the grass under the tree. She likes to sit in the dirt. We bring out an old kettle and a wooden spoon and Maddie fills the pot full of stones and grass and dirt and then we put in water from the hose. She stirs and stirs. "Soup!" I say, or "Birthday cake!" I say, and pretend to eat some off the spoon. Maddie watches this very seriously. I don't know whether she is afraid I'm really eating it or afraid I'm really not.

Irene is coming again. We are going out for lunch and Dot is watching the baby which makes her so happy that she doesn't say anything mean about Irene. We are going to the pet store because I am thinking about buying a dog for Buddy. And I think Old Dog would like some company on the porch, I have heard it keeps you young to have a puppy around and Old Dog could use a shot of youth. One of his eyes is all milky and the other gets gummed up so you have to swab it with a piece of Kleenex. This is disgusting at first but you get used to it. Irene thinks a dog is a great idea and she wants to help me pick one out. Well, I can pick out my own dog thank you, but it is nice of her to give me a ride. We are going in the green truck which she calls The Beast. Irene is one of those people who names her trucks. I don't really mind Irene. I think she can be quite thoughtful and nice. The worst part about her is that she feels she needs to show off how much better she knows Buddy than I do. For instance, I don't really care if he went out three Halloweens ago as Dot.

"What did he wear?" I ask her, thinking this is strange, Dot doesn't dress oddly at all.

"He took two cartons of Tareytons and the *TV Guide*," says Irene. Well, I don't know that I think that is all that funny, to tell the truth.

Irene's fingernails are quite long. They make clicking noises on the steering wheel when she wants to make a point. "That's sort of mean, isn't it?" I say to her now.

"Oh, Virginia," says Irene. *Click click*. "It was a joke. It was my idea anyway, don't blame the Bud-boy."

The Bud-boy? What a ridiculous name.

Irene is a very good driver. She knows how to use a stick shift and everything that I could not figure out the time Buddy tried to teach me. "No, I cannot feel that," I said to him in a huff when he went on and on about the clutch like it was the damn Messiah. Irene can even parallel park which she did outside the stores in Montclair where we are shopping today. Montclair is like New York City compared to Hadley but not as nice as Wellfleet by a long shot.

Irene is wearing eyeliner as usual and eye shadow although it is broad daylight and mascara as well as lipstick. She is also wearing a straight black skirt that shows off her nice figure and a turtleneck angora sweater of sky blue even though it is quite hot. I am wearing my crummy old maternity dress from last year, which is very comfortable but I notice some stains around the tummy and what with that and my dirty sneakers I don't feel very pulled together all of a sudden.

"Don't be silly," says Irene kindly when I mention this to her. "Nobody's looking at what you have on. They're all staring at those big brown eyes of yours." Well, it is nice of her to mention that. My eyes are among my best features and it has never been necessary for me to resort to eyeliner or mascara.

"Oh, you have lovely eyes too, Irene," I say, although it is a lie, Irene's eyes are on the small side which is why she dolls them up so much. They are a nice color, though, being a dark blue.

"And you've got those cheekbones," says Irene. "People would kill for those cheekbones." I didn't think Irene noticed things like that. Nor did I ever think about my cheekbones before. I pull out my compact when Irene is distracted and I look in the mirror. All I can see, actually, is this pale face with dark circles under the eyes. And then Irene makes me buy a lipstick when what I really need is Erace.

"You need something pink," says Irene, opening one lipstick after another and testing them on the back of her wrist so that pretty soon she looks like a person with a disease. "Here." She has picked out a hot pink which she says will go well with my hair and my eyes. "I guarantee it," says Irene, "they'll be following you home if you put that on. You'll have to beat them away at the door."

"Oh, don't be silly," I say, but I try it on and I do look a bit nicer, I have to say. It gives me kind of a boost.

"You see? Come to Aunt Irene, makeup expert of the Western world," says Irene. She smiles happily. In fact, I think Irene actually likes me. We go to the perfume counter next and I try on several different scents. So does Irene. Pretty soon she squirts one at me and I squirt another at her and we are giggling away like maniacs. The saleswoman frowns at us and I say, "Come on, Irene, let's go," but Irene takes one last squirt of My Sin and then we go over to scarves.

I have to say it is a lot of fun going shopping with Irene.

"Oh, this is so beautiful," I say, taking down a Hermès scarf with a picture of a horse on it.

"Hermeez," says Irene. I feel embarrassed that she mispronounces Hermès but where would Irene learn to speak French anyway? "Jesus Mary and Joseph," says Irene, whistling at the price tag.

"These scarves are very precious," I say. "They are imported from France." And I very carefully drape it back on the stand.

"Do you mind if I try on a bathing suit?" asks Irene. "My old one is too ratty to wear. We're not in a real big hurry, are we?"

"Of course not, Irene," I say. "I'll try one on too." So we pick out a couple of bathing suits and go into this communal dressing room which embarrasses me because I am so modest. "This light is brutal," says Irene and I say, "God, I hate this," and then we start putting on our suits. I am too shy to get naked in front of anybody so I put it on under my big dress and then just hold the dress up by my shoulders to see. Irene does not laugh at me for which I am grateful. In fact she is fairly modest herself. "What do you think?" she asks, turning around and I have to look at her. This is very embarrassing since it is another human being's actual body. "Oh, I think you look terrific, Irene," I say, and she says, "How about yours?" and I say, "Oh, I'm not going to get one today," and she says, "Go get the little yellow one, go ahead, it would look good on you," so I leave and when I come back right away it surprises Irene just as she is wearing only her little underpants and bra and her stomach is a terrible mess of stretch marks. "Oh, gosh," I say, as she quickly turns around. "I'm sorry."

"Well," she says, "it's hard to knock on a dressing room curtain."

I never saw anything so bad except for this woman in the hospital when I had Maddie who had had twins. Irene must once have had a terrible weight problem. Now we are both embarrassed and Irene starts to put her sweater back on which is when I notice she has a hickey on her neck. I don't say anything to her about either thing because I was not raised to make such personal remarks. But I didn't know Chick was so passionate. Buddy used to do that to my neck. But when you're married everything sort of dies down. Irene buys a little bright red one-piece bathing suit and I don't buy the one-piece with polka dots and a skirt or the yellow one and then we go to look at puppies.

They are the cutest puppies. They are beagles and I love them but Irene says Buddy used to have a beagle named

Lefty and when it got run over he said he never wanted another beagle as long as he lived. So I wind up not getting a puppy. We look at lizards for a while and turtles (which I love) and a big snake in the back. There are a bunch of kittens too, but I don't think a kitten is a good present for Buddy. Or a rabbit, either, although Irene loves the rabbit.

So then we go have lunch.

"I still look at boys, I hate to admit it," I tell Irene when we are having our chocolate sodas. "I don't know what gets into me. I was so used to seeing if they were looking at me all my life that I still kind of check them out. It is really a terrible thing, I know it. Buddy would die if he knew. God. Don't tell. He'd get really mad." I say this because Irene has whispered that the boy in the booth across the aisle is a dead ringer for James Dean. She has stepped on my foot about it. "I know," I say. "But God. We're married, Irene! We're both married!" I am having such a good time. And I love chocolate ice cream sodas. I love the long spoons they give you.

Irene is just sitting there hunched over her glass playing with her straw. She isn't even eating her ice cream and I have already gobbled mine up. "You got married real quick," she says. "Things don't change overnight just because you get married. Besides," and she starts eating again, "besides, we've still got eyes, don't we?" Irene is so understanding, it's strange. Here I am talking to Buddy's old girlfriend like she was my oldest friend in the world.

"You know what's the good thing about being married?" I say. "I don't have to be anything now."

"How do you mean?" Irene finally eats her cherry.

"Like a teacher or anything. It's somewhat of a relief."

"I'm going to be a nurse," says Irene.

"You are? A nurse?" I am surprised. Irene already works at the Poodle-Rama as a dog groomer.

"Yeah. I'm going to go to night school."

"How can you do all that? God. Well, of course you don't have to worry about a baby," I say, and then my face gets hot and I try to smile but I feel like my teeth are big points in my face. "I mean all those sick people and everything. I couldn't do it. You have to be a strong person."

"Yeah, that hospital food can kill you." Irene laughs.

"I ate everything they brought me when I had Maddie," I say. I don't know why I keep mentioning babies every second. Partly I am somewhat jealous. She seems so set. But at least I have had a baby, the ultimate for a woman. "Have you ever been in a hospital?" I ask.

"Oh," says Irene, and she runs her hand through her hair the way she does. "I had my stomach pumped out when I was a kid. I ate a box of matches."

"Irene! I did the exact same thing!" I am so excited. "What an amazing coincidence! I ate a box of the wooden kind. But I don't remember having my stomach pumped at all."

"I do," says Irene. "The nurse held my hand."

"Oh, I know," I say, "nurses can make such a huge difference to a hospital stay."

I have noticed before that Irene is actually a very pale person like myself. Her skin is really kind of white, like mine. I usually dot my cheeks with lipstick and then rub it in. We are both pale people. And maybe what I saw on her stomach was actually just the shadows. I probably imagined the whole thing. It could have been a shadow.

I mention it to Buddy after supper. He is home, of all things.

"It's so funny, Buddy, about me and Irene. We are so similar in so many ways. We have so much in common." Buddy's head snaps up. "We both had our stomachs pumped out for eating matches when we were little. Isn't that funny?"

"Hey," he says, and his face relaxes. "Two little spitfires, huh?" he says but I can tell he is thinking only of Irene.

"Really," I say, just to keep the conversational ball rolling. "And I always wanted to be a nurse myself too." This is of course a complete lie. In fact I had no idea what I wanted to be. "I think she is a very determined person to want to be a nurse." I want Buddy to say it takes more determination to take care of a baby but that is not what he says. "Irene is a pisser" is what he says. Irene is a pisser. It is the biggest compliment I ever heard Buddy give. And I feel like he thinks I am just a not real person, as if she is much realer than I am, as if every time I open my mouth somebody puts a spoonful of pink frosting into it.

At least I'm not a damn midget and I don't wear an ankle bracelet. I walk down the street and people whistle even if I have the baby with me which I think is disgusting. I'd love to tell Buddy to see if he got jealous but he'd say it was my fault, that I must somehow be sending out the signals. What nonsense. Just because he is studying psychology he thinks he knows everything about me. That is so ridiculous. I don't even know me myself.

$\mathcal{D}$o you have anything?" Buddy asked in a hoarse voice. I didn't honestly know what he was talking about at that exact moment. "Do you want me to use something? Is it okay?"

I said it was okay.

I go back over it in my mind but I don't see what I could have done differently. I would never have said it was not okay, I'm sure of that. Not after where we'd gotten to, and how much I was sure I loved him. It was wonderful to be held so tight. Was that it? I don't know. I honestly don't know.

Today Madeline was running around outside in her birthday suit and we had the hose and I squirted her and she ran squealing around with her fat little stomach sticking out and trying to catch the stream of water in her hands and in her mouth, squealing and squealing. Old Dog came lumbering around the house and I squirted him too, but gently, and the water just ran off his back in rivulets. Then we gave him a drink in Madeline's bucket and he slopped it right up. When it gets really hot he crawls under the back steps and sleeps in the blue gravel that got put there once upon a time. In fact that's how you can tell how hot a day it is, by where Old Dog decides to collapse. He is not so bad, really.

Tonight I made pork chops and pineapple even though it was so hot and they were not very good. I don't know what I did wrong. I also made mashed potatoes which Madeline loves and peas which she spits out. I took to hiding one pea in a spoonful of mashed potatoes but she found it every time. Then she wouldn't eat the potato either. She just made this terrible little betrayed face and clamped her little lips shut. Buddy said she needs to learn to eat her peas. I said that was ridiculous. I said I'd find something else green that she liked to eat. But he tried to get her to open her mouth. "Open up, Madeline," said Buddy, frowning. "Choochoo." Of course she wouldn't, I know my little girl. If she doesn't want to open her mouth nothing will get her to. "What are you going to do, push it through her five little teeth?" I asked him. "You big strong man?" I admit I was a little sarcastic sounding, but he made me mad. You can't just come home once in a while for supper and then expect to make everybody do what you say. At least not Madeline. Then he tried pinching her cheeks to get her mouth open and she started screaming bloody murder and he popped a couple of peas in and she blew them right out again and I'm sorry to say but I laughed. He got all huffy and left the table. So it was just me and Madeline looking at each other. I swear she knows her daddy is a jerk. But it wasn't me who told her. Old Dog ate the peas and the mashed potatoes.

When I got back to my room in the dorm after I had sexual intercourse with Buddy the first thing I wanted to do was look in the mirror. I knew you changed, but I wasn't sure how I would look. I wanted to see if you could tell by my face that I knew something really deep and important now, that I was a woman, that I had experienced the ultimate in life. How much more can you know than if you give yourself utterly to a human being in sexual intercourse? You have had another person inside your body. I always imagined doing it in a meadow, of course, but it doesn't really matter where you do it. You can't always know beforehand when the first time will be. Sometimes one thing just leads to another more quickly than you thought it would.

I have to say I looked exactly the same. Maybe a little bit rabbity. I think I was probably staring too hard. I was hoping for a somewhat dreamy wise expression, but I guess you have to catch yourself off guard for that. I'm sure if I looked in a three-way mirror I could sneak up on my profile, so to speak.

My roommate was waiting up which was pretty nice of her since it was two A.M. She had a habit of knitting and then using her needles to reach down in a thin jar of pickled kumquats. She was extremely poised and a little fat. I told her, because I could swear she already knew. "We did it," I said, making my voice sound as knowledgeable as I could while still dreamy. Amy paused with a kumquat on the end of her needle halfway to her mouth. It dripped on her book, *Principles of Accounting*. "You lie," she said.

"No," I said, "don't I look different to you?"

I thought she would be more interested than she was. All she wanted to know was did we use anything. "What did you use, Virginia?" she asked.

"Well," I said. "Actually, we really didn't use anything." I would have felt so bad stopping him right in the middle like that. I just didn't think I should interrupt everything. Even though he asked.

This is what I hate. Going to the Acme with Buddy and he has to question every single thing I buy. It is either expensive or unnecessary. Vanilla, for example. Buddy says since he can't taste vanilla in anything why do we have to spend umpteen dollars on a little bottle of it? If it were up to him we would eat dented tomatoes and flea-bitten old reduced bread. "I suppose you'd like me to make soup out of your damn socks," I say, and he says, "Well, if it would get them clean," which means he is in a good mood. Buddy in a good mood puts me in a good mood. This is how it works. If he is in a bad mood and I can get him in a good mood then I feel good too for a while. If he stays in a good mood too long then I get in a bad mood. Why should he be in a good mood and I am the one stuck at home with the baby?

The Acme is not the best store but it is the only one I can walk to. Yesterday I went with Maddie because Buddy was at work and my daddy sent me fifty dollars in the mail to buy whatever I wanted just for myself. I bought a nice eye of round and some sour cream and the good kind of canned peas. I bought a lot of cereal which Buddy likes. I bought flour and coffee and butter and four kinds of cheese. I bought vanilla. I bought bitter chocolate and walnuts and eggs. And then I couldn't carry it home because it turned out I had five bags plus Madeline and I was stranded in the front of the store with no way home. I didn't know what to do. I was embarrassed so I pretended to be looking out the window for my ride which of course there was no ride. I refuse to be one of those people who takes a shopping cart out of the parking lot and walks home with it and it stays in their yard until there are five Acme shopping carts and then they have more kids and the kids play war with them and somebody comes out on the porch in his undershirt and yells with a can of beer in his hand.

So I stood there and let Maddie have an entire box of Cheerios to play with and suddenly there was Chick out of nowhere. "Shopped yourself into a corner?" he asked, and I answered, "Oh, I most certainly have," and he said, "Got Irene's truck right outside. I saw you earlier and I honked but you didn't see."

Oh. So that was Chick. I try not to look if somebody honks or whistles when I am walking for fear they will think I am in the flirting stage and would be willing to have just anybody in a car or truck slow down and stroke up a conversation. Or worse, offer me a ride. So I hadn't looked up and it was Chick! How harmless! And very nicely he drove me home. He even helped me carry the groceries into the kitchen. It is terrible that no matter how many bags you bring home by the time you put it in the cupboards and the icebox it looks like nothing at all.

Buddy is at night school three times a week now and Dot and I sit outside on the porch most evenings. There are fireflies here when it gets dark and Old Dog now and then lifts his head and tries to catch one but he is just too pathetic. "I don't know what Old Dog was good for when he was young," says Dot, shaking her head, but you know she loves him because she doesn't get up and move when he lays a tremendous fart. She just fans the air in front of her face with her magazine. My eyes water and I breathe through my nose in case molecules from inside Old Dog's bottom get in my mouth and down inside my own body. I mean, it comes from there, doesn't it? Dot is not fastidious. Her glasses are often smeary and sometimes her neck looks kind of gray, but this is from working in the yard on the weekend. She also bites her thumbnails in the evening, a sound which would drive my mother crazy, I am sure, but I have gotten almost used to it. She is trying not to smoke. She coughs and bites her thumbs and then she scrapes her chair back and goes into the kitchen and comes back with a lit cigarette. "Oh, Dot," I say, "you're not supposed to do that." I hide the matches on her after dinner but she knows how to light a cigarette even if there are no matches and the pilot light is out. She takes a straw from the broom and puts it inside the toaster and pushes the toaster down. The broom straw lights right up and Dot is very proud of herself.

Dot and I saw a loose chicken today and we don't know whose it was. We were sitting in the yard and it came running across the grass and Old Dog startled and got up and tried to run after it but the chicken was faster than he was and it was so comical to see him give up and come flop back down on the porch. He kept growling little cover-up growls, as if to say, Look out Mr. Chicken! And every so often he'd lift his head and look around and give a little warning bark. The worst thing I ever saw that had to do with chickens was a row of them hanging by their feet in a barn next door to somewhere we used to live. There were about fifteen chickens hanging upside down with little slits cut in their throats and they were bleeding to death that way but they were still very much alive, and the other chickens were standing around drinking the blood from their fellow chickens' throats. We were horrified, me and the other kids. We wanted to untie their feet but we couldn't, and we knew the chickens were done for anyway, what with the holes in their throats, and we wound up hating the other chickens more than we hated the farmer.

"My mama would've just wrung that bird's neck and plucked it clean in no time and we'd have ourselves a nice chicken dinner," says Dot tonight. We are sitting outside on the porch and all the lights in the house are off except the one small one in the living room. Maddie is fast asleep and Buddy isn't home. "Me," says Dot, "I don't want to see a piece of chicken unless it's already battered up and fried and in the paper bag hot for me to eat it. Just goes to show," says Dot.

"Oh," I say, "I think it would be fun to make a chicken dinner but I could never kill a living thing." This is true. I don't even like to swat flies.

"Honey," says Dot, "only one neck I'd like to wring about now," and she laughs and rocks and the chair squeaks the boards on the old porch. She means Buddy, of course, who is so late we had to put his dinner away in the icebox. He is out late most of the time. We almost never see him when he is awake anymore. It is true that he is working hard all day plus night school, but it is funny to think I almost don't have a husband at all.

"Well, blow me down," says Dot, "speak of the devil," as Buddy pulls in the driveway. "Where have you been?" asks Dot. She is tapping her watch.

"Library," Buddy says, climbing the porch steps. "I was at the library." He looks around at the two of us who are like great stone faces. "You want me to pass, don't you?" He says this in a kidding serious voice. So I know he knows he was wrong.

"What library?" I ask.

"Downtown," says Buddy.

"It's open this late?" I can't help asking. He is standing by Dot's rocker with his hand on the back of her chair. He is wearing a red checked shirt and his hair is so dark and beautiful I would like to smack him.

"Went out for a beer with the guys," says Buddy, giving

Dot's chair a playful little rock, and then he goes inside and snaps on the kitchen light as if he were the king of everyone.

Sometimes I wish he would never come home. Sometimes I think Dot and I could be very happy sitting here by ourselves. Of course, it would be nice to be always expecting him, but okay if he never showed up for the rest of our lives. He spoils the nice quiet mood we get ourselves into. It can be very peaceful just sitting on the porch in the dark and then his car crunches up the driveway and doors start slamming and all these sudden noises hurt my skin.

"Any pie left?" he calls. It makes me feel good that he wants pie. I wish I didn't care whether he wants a piece of damn pie or not.

"In the icebox on the bottom shelf," I say, "wrapped up in wax paper." I hear the door open and close. I hear him get a plate out of the cupboard. He comes outside with his plate and sits on the step next to Old Dog. Old Dog raises his head and Buddy gives him a bite of pie. Buddy loves Old Dog too.

"Good pie," says Buddy. Chew chew. "You make this, Virginia?"

"Yes," I say. My whole self is perched for happiness.

"Your wife is some kind of cook," says Dot, but Buddy's mouth is too full to talk. His fork makes little clinks on the plate.

"Good pie. Nice night." And he looks at the sky. Then he gets up and goes back into the kitchen where I hear him rinse the plate.

"I'm turning in," calls Buddy through the screen.

"Well," says Dot, "it's been nice seeing you." I can hear she's ticked off at him.

"Oh, good night, Buddy," I say.

"Good night," he calls.

"Night," says Dot.

"Night," I say.

"That boy is working too hard," says Dot, getting up from the chair. "You got to see that he comes home earlier." I don't know what she thinks she means by this. She knows I don't have any say in what Buddy does. I wish she wouldn't talk as if I had any influence on him.

"Oh, sure thing," I say, but I am mad.

"I know it's hard, honey," says Dot, "but you're his wife." It scares me when she talks like this. As if she didn't understand one thing I know, or as if she knows something I don't.

But the thing is, I don't even want it. I don't know what I want. But I don't want this. And the worst thing is sometimes when he is late I get to thinking maybe he has died in a car crash. Or maybe he has sawn his own head off in a terrible accident at work. And this terrible little feeling of joy shoots through me.

One time Buddy wanted to try something that I didn't want to try. Some things are private. He acted like there was something wrong with me just because I didn't want to do what he wanted to do. "This has got to feel good, Virginia," he said to me, and he sounded exasperated and tired out. But I don't see how one person can decide that for another person. "What is wrong with you?" he said. Well. There is nothing whatsoever wrong with me. I am a different human being from him, that's what is so-called wrong with me. Let him go find a dog to do that with, is what I felt like saying. "Go kiss somebody else's hiney." Buddy does not like the word "hiney." I usually use the word "bottom" but it doesn't sound like a grown-up wife. "Hiney" is the only other word I actually like. "Ass" is too vulgar sounding. And I despise the word "butt." It sounds so hard and calloused to me. And bottoms are usually softer. Not Buddy's, of course. He has practically no ass whatsoever. To use his word.

These days I am so glad to get into bed and know that he won't be wanting to stick his damn tongue in my mouth. The thought of it makes me want to scream. And I don't understand why. I used to love it. There used to be lots of things I liked. Once upon a time I could spend hours just making out and never get tired of it. But now I feel like you have to go to so much trouble, and it just isn't worth it.

Sometimes I do what I call have a daydream. It is always about Rock Hudson and I do it in the bed with the shades pulled down. Sometimes I am afraid what if I died in this position? Would everyone know what I had been doing? It would be so embarrassing. Or could I just before I died realize that I was having a heart attack or something and move my hands away? I hope so. Now when I do it I always think, Now if you start to die, just move your hands a little bit and nobody will know. But this is all a total secret. Suppose Maddie ever found out that her mother died while in the midst of this practice?

If I did die, I wonder if Buddy would instantly marry Irene. They would raise Maddie up as if she were their child. I keep thinking about Irene's stomach. She turned away so fast when she saw me.

Buddy comes home very tired most of the time and just falls asleep. He flips on the news and lies down on the floor and falls asleep. I say, "Buddy, why don't you sit in the chair? Why don't you go lie down on the bed? Why don't you take a shower?" Nothing works. He never pays any attention to anything I say. So of course then the rest of the night I have to step over him.

He's gone almost every night now what with one thing and another. Chick came by the other evening. Buddy was already at class. "Hey, Virginia," he said, but I didn't think to open the screen door. "Buddy's out," I told him, "as usual," I added, because I'm getting mean in my old age.

But Chick stood there anyway. The porch light was attracting bugs and he brushed a moth away from his face. "Can I come in anyway?" he asked. "Well, of course, Chick," I said, but I couldn't imagine why he was here. He looked around the kitchen as if he'd never seen it before. He touched the red placemat and the napkin ring with Buddy's napkin in it. He picked the top off the sugar bowl and put it back again gently. "I got that at the flea market," I said. "Fifty cents. Want some iced tea?"

"You fixed the place up nice, Virginia," said Chick, nodding. "Nice and cozy."

"Well, it's really Dot's kitchen," I said, "to be truthful." Although I do like to put up a few nice pictures so there is a poster of the famous lily pond by Monet over the sink and another one of Notre Dame in the hall by the telephone. I found these both at the flea market. Two dollars apiece including the frames which Dot said were quite old, maybe thirty or forty years old.

"Well," said Chick, staring at my apron which is new with red and white checks. "You added something. I don't know." This is just so typical of Chick not to notice that there is art on the walls now, not just pictures cut out from magazines of pies and cakes and Thanksgiving turkeys which is what Dot likes. It is so funny, too, because Dot is a terrible cook.

"Why, thank you, Chick," I said, surprised. That was very nice of him to say. "Some people don't notice anything," I said, meaning Buddy, of course.

"Oh," said Chick quickly. "Irene's working three days a week now and taking classes at night. I guess you could say she's pretty busy right now." He looked glum.

Well, I didn't know Irene was taking classes this summer and my skin got cold and clammy. Suppose she and Buddy were meeting every time they went to so-called school? I thought I'd faint dead away. Luckily Maddie began to stir, she has a little sniffle and I heard those snorts she makes when she's starting to wake up. I went to the fridge and took out a bottle. I set a pan of water on the stove to warm and put the bottle in it. "Keep an eye on that, Chickie, will you?" I asked and went to get the baby. I always feel better when I'm holding her even if I'm upset. I picked her right up out of the crib although she wasn't really waked up. I just wanted to hold her. I love how warm and heavy she is inside her little nightgown and she feels so good against my shoulder.

I sat down with Maddie and her bottle. "What's Irene taking?" I asked after a minute.

"Bookkeeping." Chick stared at Maddie's little feet. "I think."

"Bookkeeping!" I said, all relieved. "How hard!" Buddy is taking abnormal psych.

"Yeah," said Chick. "I know."

I was sorry I had brought it up. Irene was yelling at him last week in the Acme because he forgot to deposit his paycheck and they were overdrawn. I was there when she got so mad at him and I was very sorry to have heard it. We had just turned into the coffee aisle and Buddy was holding Madeline on his shoulders and she was pulling on his ears and squealing and biting his hair and Buddy was smooching on her feet. Then there were Chick and Irene standing in front of the Maxwell House and Irene stared at us like we were strangers and she started right in on Chick who had forgotten his wallet and it seemed they couldn't write any checks for two days and Irene only had four dollars left over from fixing the truck. We heard every word of it, it was like aimed at our direction almost. "I'm sorry, Irene," said Chick. "Really. But there's no need to get so het up about it." I had never heard anybody actually say "het up" before. Buddy looked uncomfortable. I didn't know what to do.

"What the hell are you staring at, Buddy-boy?" Irene snapped and Buddy opened his mouth to say something but closed it again. Chick trailed off after Irene down the aisle and Buddy paid for our stuff and we got out of there.

Tonight I had an example of how insane Chick can be.

He told me he wants to let a bus run over his foot. He told me he has always wanted to try it. He thinks it would feel good. "So intense," he says, "just pressed like that against the asphalt."

"Chickie." I looked him straight in the eye. "Promise me you're kidding, right? Promise me you'd never do such a crazy thing. It would be really bad." But he wouldn't promise.

"There are eighty-seven bones in the human foot," he said instead. I believe there are quite a few more. I almost let him hold the baby but decided not to. Who knows what crazy vibrations might jump from him to Madeline? He was very nice to her, though, and he tickled her feet. I never really talked to Chick before. I don't know what his real name is and I'm afraid to ask him. Suppose his real name is Chick?

Before he left I wanted to tell him I don't understand at all about the bank but thought I shouldn't mention it. He was aiming an imaginary rifle at the ceiling and firing off a few bullets. He does this when he's nervous. He would never kill a duck, though, we had a discussion about it once. He would never kill a duck or a deer or anything like that. He doesn't even really enjoy fishing. When I got up to get some cream I noticed he has a cowlick on the top of his head. Two of them, in fact. I never thought any part of Chick could be cute but cowlicks are so sweet, really. I don't know why I never noticed them before. After a while he left. I still don't know what he came over for.

Dot came by later to say good night. "Was that Chick Freund's car I saw a while ago?" she asked.

"Uh-huh," I said. I was sleepy and already in my nightgown. Dot was wearing her old pink bathrobe and no slippers. Her apartment is just back of the house. She had a million pink curlers in her hair. It is so terrible because her hair always comes out straight anyway.

"What did he want?"

"I don't know," I said. Which I did not.

"Where's Buddy?" she asked.

"I don't know," I said. "Class."

"Everything all right over here?" asked Dot. She seemed suspicious all of a sudden as if she wanted to look under the bed, or in the closet. She kept picking up the cups and plates and she even picked up the bunch of bananas and looked in the bowl as if somebody might be hiding underneath.

"What do you mean?" I said. "Of course everything is all right. Why wouldn't it be all right?" Why should I tell Dot that Buddy is never home. She would not say one thing except be patient with him. I know her. I am being patient. This is as patient as I know how to be. Besides, what else can I do except throw things at him?

But Dot just shook her head.

ℋow long did Irene and Buddy go out?" I ask Dot the next day.

"Whatever do you ask that for, hon?" says Dot. We are drinking our afternoon iced tea.

"Just wondering. I wondered how long, that's all."

"On and off for a couple, three years. Long time ago."

"Actually," and I take a deep breath, "actually, Dot, I was wondering if she was ever really terribly fat. She just seems like the type who might once have had a weight problem of some sort. I noticed once her stomach looked so full of stretch marks. You know what I mean?" Dot's face is a worried blank, if such a thing is possible. A worried blank. Maybe Dot does not know the meaning of stretch marks. She has never had a baby herself and she has always weighed exactly ninety-eight pounds. "I know this sounds ridiculous but I keep not knowing if maybe Irene was either tremendously fat or if possibly she might have had a baby once."

"Whatever put such a notion into your head?" Dot shakes her head now and a bobby pin goes flying off. "Don't stuff your head with nonsense, Virginia. Who have you been talking to?" Dot isn't looking at me, she is putting cookies on a plate for us.

"Nobody."

"Irene doesn't interest me. This is the only subject that interests me," says Dot, patting Madeline's head.

I have to agree with her on that. Maddie is the most beautiful baby in the world. I must have imagined the whole thing. Maybe it was the bad light in the dressing room.

"But did she?" I ask Dot a minute later.

"Did she what? Who?"

"Did Irene ever have a baby?"

"Now why would you ask a silly thing like that?" says Dot, but in a much calmer voice. "Now that I think back it seems Irene was always fighting her weight."

The first day of every new month you are supposed to say "Rabbit rabbit" before you say anything else. I cannot get Buddy to do this. I don't see why he can't oblige me on these small important matters. It is such an easy thing to do. "Where are my socks?" says Buddy. "Where's the comb?" He didn't even eat fish on New Year's Day which everybody knows is good luck. Buddy ate a cream cheese and jelly sandwich.

Dot has bought something new for Maddie and it comes in a big white box. Maddie can't open the box by herself so I take the top off and Maddie reaches in and first she pulls out little fistfuls of tissue paper which she likes very much. She looks around at us very seriously, a bunch of pink tissue paper in either hand. "There's more, Madeline," I tell her. "More! Look in the box!" She leans over and peers inside. "Ohhh," I say.

"Ohhh," says Maddie and she pulls out a darling pink hat with a big pink satin bow right in front. She puts it right on top of her head and looks at us. "Like it, like it," says Maddie.

"Oh, you look so pretty," says Dot.

"You really do," I say. "Say thank you to Dot," I say.

"Soo-soo," says Maddie.

"Dot, that is just the prettiest thing I ever saw," I say, truthfully. "But you shouldn't have spent so much money! I just know a hat like that must cost a fortune."

"Well, it's worth it if it puts a smile on your pretty face, Virginia," says Dot, which makes me burst into tears for no reason. It is so ridiculous. Then I look at Madeline who looks like a little flapper or something with the beautiful pink satin bow already crooked on her head and I can't describe how cute she is. I can't describe how I feel when I look at her, as if everything inside me were suddenly curly.

Maddie won't take her hat off. She wears it everywhere. She wants to take it into bed with her at night. Soon the bow looks a bit grimy but we have decided to let her have as much pleasure out of it as she can, me and Dot. "Either every day is a special occasion or every day is a piece of you-know-what," is Dot's theory of life.

Last night we were supposed to go out for supper, just me and Buddy, and who is there already? Irene and Chick, who looks like a sad sack. Chick and Irene do not seem to be getting along so well. I mentioned this to Buddy. He said he hadn't noticed. Well, that's a lie. I know for a fact he never takes his eyes off Irene if we run into her. And when she's cross with Chick I recognize Buddy's little smile as the smile of a person who thinks there is some hope for himself in the love department. I can tell Chick is upset. He looks unhappily over at me. It isn't like they're even touching each other. Buddy and I are on one side of the blue booth and they are on the other. It's just that Buddy and Irene only talk to each other. Chick and I might as well be on the planet Mars. "Remember that time down the shore?" Irene might begin, and Buddy will say, "Which time?" and Irene says, "The girl in the red bathing cap? That time?" and they both go into spasms of laughter while Chick and I just stare at each other. Or "Remember that time with the ducks?"

Har har har. I finally said it. "Har har hardeehar har," I said. Folding up my napkin.

Everybody looked at me. So I said it again. I had their attention finally.

"Har har har. It's so funny I forgot to laugh." I realize this was childish of me but after all, they never let us in on anything.

"What's up your ass?" asked Buddy.

"Buddy!" said Irene. "That was rude!" You could tell she meant it. Well, that was nice of her but I can fight my own battles. But then she reached across and slapped his hand and that made it into another joke. He was holding a spoon with sugar and it went all over. "Hey," he said, but you could see he loved it. I wanted to squeeze the ketchup into his eyes.

"Nothing is up my ass as you so crudely put it, but I would like to go home now. I am sure Maddie is up. In case you have forgotten in all your interesting reminiscing, you have a daughter, and she just might want to see her parents once in a while." This was ridiculous. I know it. I am always home of course. She sees us all the time. Or me, anyway. Plus it was me who wanted to go out in the first place.

"You want to leave?" said Buddy, looking all mad. "What gets into you, Virginia? We're all sitting around having a nice time and suddenly you want to leave? How about you, Irene, you want to leave? Chick? How about you?" Buddy's eyebrows were doing that thunderbolt thing on his forehead. You expect sparks to come out of his head. Chick was staring into his glass of water, poking the ice around with his thumb. Then he looked up at Buddy and he looked peculiar, like a grown-up, sort of. He had the funniest look on his face.

"Well," said Chick, whom I now love, "I was thinking

about turning in myself." Then he spoke to me as if I were a genuine person with feelings and rights. "I can give you a lift home, Virginia, if you want."

Well, I got out of the booth and took my hat off the pole and we left together. I didn't even say good-bye to Buddy or Irene. Chick's car smelled like old apple cores. "This is very nice of you, Chick," I said, very formally.

"Don't mention it," said Chick. "My pleasure."

"I hope you don't think I was too rude just now," I said. That wasn't really what I meant. I didn't think I was being rude at all, but I had to say it that way to feel Chick out.

"Buddy can be a real horse's ass," said Chick.

"Well, thank you for saying that," I said. "He can, can't he?" Chick didn't reply. I thought maybe I should say something about Irene. "It was nice of Irene to tell Buddy he was rude. Please thank her for me." I didn't exactly mean that, either. The last person I want on my side is Irene.

"Tell her yourself," said Chick, with a funny edge in his voice. I hope I didn't hurt his feelings in any way. It was a short drive to our house so we didn't say anything else. "Thank you so much," I said, getting out. I felt quite nice again. I felt like a lady. I felt as if I were wearing a really nice gray suit and high heels and stockings. That's how it made me feel, and that my hair was brushed. Not just in my old seersucker former maternity dress.

"Sweet dreams," said Chick when I got out of the car. I thought that was very nice of him.

"You too, Chick," I said, "sweet dreams to you too."

And then later I felt so angry because it took Buddy hours and hours to come home. I almost called Chick. I picked up the phone and then put it down. It rang two seconds later. It was Buddy. "I'll be home in twenty minutes," he said. But of course he wasn't. I don't know what time he got in because I was asleep. He slept on the couch anyway.

Dot always winks at me on Sunday mornings if we get up late. I know she thinks we've been in there "having a party" as she puts it. I think she thinks we are always doing it. She would be so surprised to find out the last time was March and that was the first time since November. And I really am glad. I really don't care. When I mentioned it to Buddy he said he didn't like to feel any pressure. It had to happen spontaneously, he said, and he didn't like feeling as if he had to all the time just because we were married. "Well, good," I said, "because I don't feel like it either." Of course that hurt his damn feelings, I guess, because he didn't want to talk about it ever again. I never knew boys were so sensitive. They seem to be most sensitive about their own feelings though, I have to say. Actually, I don't see how we ever did it at all. If I think about it now it's like we were two completely different people, not Buddy and Virginia at all, but two completely different people who were much nicer than we have turned out to be in actual life. And anyway, it's not really all that interesting after you're married. In fact, half the time you're just waiting for it to be over. It is so boring, really. You want to drum your fingers on the bed while you're waiting. I laughed in the middle once and Buddy got sore. "What's so funny?" he wanted to know, acting all mad. "Nothing," I said. "Really. Go on. Nothing." How could I tell him I was imagining I was reading a book with my left hand over his shoulder with the light from our clock radio? And thinking he would never know and I could get a lot of reading done this way? I couldn't say that, it would have hurt his feelings. They need to think you are paying attention to what they are doing. But sometimes your mind just wanders away.

Once I coughed and his penis came out. He got really angry over that and wouldn't speak to me for the whole next day. I say that is just ridiculous. Nature is nature, I kept saying. Maybe he thinks his is too little. Maybe that's the root of his problems. All that penis envy I think is really meant for the man. I certainly wouldn't want one. But they all want big ones. You can tell from the way they talk when they don't think you're listening. "Wait till she sees what I've got for her, snicker snicker," and so forth. I heard that kind of talk when I was in high school when nobody knew I was around. I heard Larry Gester say it to Monte Richards. It made me feel very funny, actually. But now I see it's really nothing at all. Of course Buddy would blame me for all this. He would say it is my fault that I don't enjoy the pleasures of the body and there is something the matter with me. Well, that is ridiculous. I certainly used to, that's all I can say. At least part of the body. The upper half.

I don't actually spit over my left shoulder if I see a cross-eyed woman because it would be too rude and noticeable. I simply turn my head slightly to the left and make a small *pfft* sound with my tongue. I don't think you have to actually spit. There is a cross-eyed redheaded woman whom I sometimes see in Hadley. I would not want to be cross-eyed but a harelip or a cleft palate would be the worst. I found a book in the garage, *Pye's Surgical Textbook*. It fell open to this little boy who had had an operation for a harelip and a cleft palate. The stitches were huge and messy, and it looked like somebody had sewn a barbed wire fence right into his own little face, and he knew it and was afraid to move. Every time I feel bad I open the book and look at his picture because whatever I'm feeling I feel worse for him. I want to put my arms around him and tell him it will be all right. Of course, maybe it wasn't all right. He is all grown up now since this is an old book and whatever happened to him has already happened.

𝓘rene and Chick had us over and Irene had an herbal cigarette, as she called it, which I realized after a minute was
marijuana which is an illegal drug. I was so shocked.
"You're not going to smoke that, are you?" I asked. I was
completely horrified, and she lit it right up. It smelled sick-
ening. "Buddy, you're not going to smoke that, are you?" I
said. But he just reached over to Irene for it like he'd been
doing it all his life which I am sure he has not, and he took a
big drag and then he coughed like a maniac and choked and
sputtered and I said, "That is not particularly attractive," as
he hacked away, and then I left the room. I felt like a spoiled
princess with a long train dragging on the floor and I went
outside on the porch and sat on the swing. Pretty soon they
were all laughing away in there, even Chick. What if somebody heard? What if somebody called the police? It was
very dangerous and stupid and illegal and I couldn't stand
that this was actually happening in my presence. I went
back into the living room and plopped down on the sofa
next to Chick. "You are doing something really wrong," I
said, "and I think you should stop. I think you should stop
and stop laughing so loud. Somebody is going to wonder
what's going on in here."

"Want a hit?" asked Irene nicely, her eyes sort of swollen
and funny looking.

"I don't think so," I said, and I folded my arms. "I'm just
in here to see what's going on. God knows what might

happen." The air smelled sweet and peculiar and it smelled really illegal, I don't know how else to put it. But pretty soon I had an interesting idea. "What is everybody's favorite breakfast?" It is what I like to know about people, I don't know why. I just always like to know what everybody eats for breakfast. I'm just naturally interested and tonight I decided to ask everybody. It seemed like a good time to ask. I went first. "Mine is pancakes and maple syrup and sausages and coffee."

"You never eat that," said Buddy. His eyes were red too, but he looked really friendly although not in a personal way. Like if you snapped his picture you'd think here was a friendly guy.

"I said favorite breakfast. Not what you necessarily eat. But that too," I said. "I actually mostly eat coffee and two pieces of toast with butter and marmalade. Chick?" I asked, indicating that he should go next. I thought we should go around the room clockwise. I was so glad to be having a civilized conversation.

"Root beer."

"I beg your pardon?"

"I like root beer for breakfast. And I drink root beer for breakfast. That's it." Chick looked embarrassed. He wasn't very good at this. I couldn't believe my ears, actually.

"Chick. You mean to tell me you drink a soft drink for breakfast and that's all you have? That's terrible."

"I like it," said Chick. He was wearing a red plaid shirt and jeans. He didn't have any shoes on and he was wiggling his toes in his socks.

"I like a cup of tea with honey and lemon and scrambled eggs hard," said Irene. "Real hard." And she burst out laughing. I didn't see what was so funny, really. Buddy rocked back and forth laughing. He slapped his thigh. Who is this person? I thought.

"But I just drink a Coke," said Irene, wiping her eyes.

"What?" I asked.

Irene nodded.

"I can't get into this," said Buddy. It was his turn. "Anyway, you know what I like."

For some reason this made Irene laugh more. Buddy blushed and so did Chick.

"No, I do not," I said. "What do you like?" I said this in as cold a voice as possible. "I only know what you eat which is a cup of coffee. I do not know what you like. We have never discussed this issue before."

"Pussy," said Irene, just as loud and clear as anything. "First thing in the morning for breakfast. Get the day off to a good start. Pussy."

Well, I got right up and left the room. I started walking home. We do not live more than six blocks from their place and I was not going to spend another second under that roof.

"She was kidding," said Buddy, who came running after me. "Irene has a warped sense of humor." But I did not speak to him even though he followed me all the way home. All I said was, "Don't you touch me." I heard him explaining to Dot that I had a stomach cramp and that was why I went right in and locked myself in the bathroom. "You know how modest she is," I heard Buddy say, as if he knew himself even one damn thing about me. I slept in the living room on the sofa with Old Dog snoring away on the rug.

$\mathcal{I}$'m real sorry I spoke out of turn," said Irene. She called me the next day. "Really, Virginia," she said, "it was the grass. I swear I'm sorry. I was only joking, honest. Cross my heart and hope to die. Sometimes I just disgust myself. Really."

"Well, thank you very much for calling," I said. I didn't feel like myself. I felt a very great distance from my actual body and it was beginning to worry me. I sat down on the chair and held on to the arms and I thought, Something is the matter with me but I don't know what it is. I don't feel like myself. But of course how could I? I don't even know who myself is! That should have made me laugh at least for a second but it didn't. It made me scared. What if I turned out to be like a murderer? What if nobody was safe in the same house with me? If I didn't know who I was or what I was going to do, then it could be anything or anybody, couldn't it? Suppose I turned out to be really crazy and Buddy woke up with a knife in his heart? For the whole morning I sat like that until finally Madeline woke up and I went to get her and changed her and talked to her and did the normal things a normal person does. But I didn't feel normal. I looked in the mirror to see if I looked different. I looked exactly the same. So that was one good thing, that nobody would know what crazy thoughts I was actually having. God. And I couldn't think of one person to tell on the earth. Not even my own mother. She would say to get my mind off myself. It is my mother's belief that most people's problems come from thinking too hard about themselves. She says the best thing is to take down a book and learn something new. She would not understand that there are times when you can't even get up from the chair, I am sorry to say. She is quite strong. I am not that strong, as it turns out. I seem to be somewhat of a weak person.

"Hello you darling," I said to Madeline, "Mommy's darling girl," and then I just cried into her neck. I couldn't help it. I know it was wrong of me but I couldn't stop for one minute. "Silly Mommy," I finally said. "Silly silly Mommy." She looked at me so seriously. I kissed her face a thousand times and I made a big nest on the living room floor out of the pillows off everything and I put a sheet over the top of us like a tent. I invited Old Dog in too and he just flopped down and breathed heavy. He only smelled like wet hair not terrible smells. We were like birds in a nest under a canopy and Maddie loved it. I made whistling noises like hurricane winds and we had to get snuggly and stay safe. I love that game and so does Madeline. I didn't do anything else all day except sit there in the nest. Buddy came home for supper which was a novelty and I threw a bunch of frozen hamburger in the pan without even trying. He said it didn't matter, he had a sinus condition today and couldn't taste a thing. He said this to be nice, I know. I detest the word "sinus" when I am sitting at the table even if it is just old horrible hamburger. I detest the word "sinus" which sounds all prissy and whiny, and it makes you think of the word "cavity" which is extremely unattractive when used about the human body. Sinus cavity, how disgusting. Big empty stomachs and bladders floating around, not to mention uterus which sounds so tough and chewy. What with one thing and another we did not eat much dinner.

Well, sweetie," said Amy. "You're an idiot." We had just figured out that the night was the fourteenth day of a twenty-eight-day cycle. "He nailed you on the fourteenth day of a twenty-eight-day cycle?" she repeated, which was not necessary since I had just said it myself. "Brace yourself," she said. "You might easily be pregnant."

"Oh, no," I said, "I'm sure that wouldn't happen." But I

was experiencing the exact feeling of cold feet. Both my feet were suddenly as cold as stones.

"It wouldn't happen?" Amy ate a kumquat. She put the whole thing in her mouth. Juice dribbled down her chin and I started laughing. Really. She laughed too. It was the only thing to do, actually, under the circumstances.

It seems so funny to remember those days. It wasn't even that long ago. It was as if everything suddenly got covered with this thin layer of ice and if you moved, your skin would break.

By the time Buddy got home the next night I had made nests all over the house. We had one in the living room made out of two sheets and the bedspread which was held up by the backs of chairs and the broom in the middle like a tent pole. We had pillows in there. In the bedroom I made one out of Maddie's crib and the bureau and a chair and this was done with the old blue blanket so it was hot but we could sit under that one too. In the kitchen I put an old sheet over the table plus three tablecloths and these hung down over the sides and drooped to the floor and we could sit under the table there too and hold our breath. The best place for Old Dog was the living room tent which allowed for his bad smells. We were sitting in the living room tent eating our supper when Buddy came in. "What the hell is going on?" he roared. "Shhh," I said to Maddie.

"Virginia?" He sounded angry and worried. "Virginia? What's going on here?" He was in the living room and I could see his shoes under the tent. We held our breath and then I began to giggle and whooosh, he pulled off the sheets.

"Oh, hi," I said.

Part Two

So now here I am again in my own bed in Wellfleet because it was decided I needed a vacation. The stresses were too much and Buddy had exams coming up. My daddy called up and said, "We miss you, Virginia, come on home with the baby for a while," and he sent me money for the train. I am sure Dot called and said I wasn't feeling well. I am happy to be here although it is a strange feeling to be home with my baby where everything has changed at the same time everything is the same. The furniture looks bigger to me. Or smaller, I can't decide. Even the space around the furniture looks different from the way it used to. Maddie loves to burrow under the cushions on the flowered sofa, you can see the little pink soles of her feet. "Boo!" says Maddie from under the cushions. "Boo!" Our house smells the same, mothballs and applesauce.

My mother has not been well, it turns out. Daddy never tells me things until they are over, which upsets me. I would like to help. I hate thinking I was just going about my business in Hadley with my own selfish problems while my mother was having a minor operation. "I didn't want to worry you, Virginia," says my daddy. He pats my shoulder. But I know he just needs to keep his problems to himself or worse, ask God's help. I am sorry to say I do not believe for one instant in the Christian religion. I just don't believe there is a god like that up there looking down at us. In this regard I am more like my mother. She gets fidgety in church and no longer goes except on the big holidays even though she is the minister's wife. She gets dizzy and sick to her stomach and Ladies' Auxiliary bring her things instead of the other way around. She was never meant to be a minister's wife anyway. When she married my daddy he was on his way to being a doctor, then he got the calling. God just tapped him on the shoulder like someone cutting in at a dance. And Daddy had to follow. So my mother thought she was marrying a medical man but overnight he turned into a minister. "I am not cut out for this role," she has said time and again, the role of the minister's wife. He can't argue with her, of course. She never said she was. Of course she loves him anyway, she always has. "Herbert," I have heard her say one million times, "Herbert, *je t'aime.*" My father writes all his own sermons. Some people send away for sermons to read but Daddy writes all his own. He is a highly educated man. Mother was glad when we moved here where people have heard of William Wordsworth for a change. We have lived many places where people love to talk about "pinky rings," which is one of my mother's pet peeves in the word department. Places where nobody can even recite "To be or not to be, that is the question." Shakespeare is not a personal favorite of my mother's, she calls him "the other William," but she acknowledges his place in literature.

"Hello, Mother," I say, tiptoeing into her room. It is so gray and still in here, like church. Her room always reminds me of church not because of Daddy, but because you aren't allowed to touch anything. You can't sit on the bed unless she invites you, and you can't sit down at her dressing table and play with her lipsticks and powder, and you can't open her drawers and touch her things. She would just kill you with a look. It works as well as if she had little tiny poisonous snakes in there. She is getting better. They found a lump under her arm which turned out to be nothing at all, but it gave my daddy a good scare. I don't know if it scared my mother as she would never care to discuss anything so personal. "Hello," I say again, because she hasn't turned in her bed to look at me. She just lies there. From her breathing I think she is awake but you don't push yourself on my mother. "I'll come back later," I whisper, and back out of the room. You have to allow her her privacy. My mother is a private and dignified person.

"Your mother hasn't been well," is what Daddy said to me, "although she is going to be fine."

"Oh, Daddy," I said, and I patted his arm because he was sort of crying. "Oh, Daddy, what happened?" I was scared now too, as I have hardly ever seen my daddy lose control of his emotions in a negative way. He shook his head. I had to wait for a couple of minutes while he pulled himself together which he did by turning his back to me and looking out the window.

Daddy gets his inspiration and comfort from nature. It works for him even in the dead of winter. He has preached that he even loves the bare trees shorn of life because they remind him of our Saviour. His saviour, not mine or my mother's. We have not got Daddy's faith. On Saturdays when he writes his sermons and listens to his music my mother and I just sit outside the study door and mope. Or she slaps her thigh or bangs things around. She does not like to play second fiddle to God. My father listens to opera frequently but my mother prefers show tunes and this is another sore spot between them. Other than that, my parents are as in love with each other now as on the first day they met. This is the source of all my security. My parents love each other more than anything on earth. I know it is possible to marry and remain in love forever.

It is just not happening to me.

Maddie loves my daddy. She gets on his lap and goes after all the pencils and pens he keeps in his shirt pocket. He lets her take them by pretending to stare at the ceiling while she grabs them and starts taking the tops off and he cries, "Oh no!" and she just laughs and laughs, her little chin digs into her front and she laughs so hard she gets the hiccups. It is funny to watch and makes me very happy. "Pop-Pop!" says Maddie. "More! More!" and he puts the pens back and it starts all over. Soon my mother comes out of the bedroom in her dressing gown and says, "I thought I heard a commotion in here," and she brushes away our worried looks and sits down on the sofa next to Daddy and I hope and pray Maddie will want to sit on her lap and she does. Thank God. It really hurts her feelings when Maddie doesn't want her and I never know what to do or say. Except for those moments we are sort of like one big happy family.

Fortunately nobody asks me what I am doing home, and how I was acting before I came. Nobody is saying, Why were you making all those nests? Because I don't know what I would answer. Here I have not made one nest or even thought about it. I hardly ever think about Buddy and I never worry about what he is doing which is strange but true nonetheless. Out of sight out of mind is what is happening to me.

My mother is up a little longer each day. Pretty soon she will feel strong enough to go out for lunch. She is looking forward to that greatly. Meanwhile, I run all the errands. Sometimes she takes care of Maddie for me, whenever Daddy is in the house too, in case it gets to be too much for her because although she swears she is now as strong as ever I see her wince when she picks up Maddie's little shoe from the floor. I try to keep everything shipshape so she has nothing to do.

My mother is a neat woman. I used to peek in her dresser when she was out, feeling like a criminal because I know how she values her privacy. Even now I keep thinking I could find some huge secret in there, something that has to do with everything but all there is is underwear in a silky bag, and stockings inside stockings inside another silky bag, and gloves in a glove box. Everything is inside something else. Nothing just lies around loose. "What are you doing!" she said once, surprising me by coming home early and quietly opening the door. I was in her top drawer looking for lipstick. "Oh!" I said, like a crook. "I was hoping to borrow a pair of gloves!" which was of course a lie. She came over and pushed the drawer shut hard. "You do not go into other people's things, Virginia. You ask first." What is the point of asking when all you'll get is a lecture? It is just not worth it. On top of that if you use her hairbrush you have to pull out all your hair and replace the brush exactly where she keeps it or she knows. My mother is exact about the possessions on her dressing table. I used to sit there and use her three-way mirror to stare at my face from all directions, looking for clues as to who I might actually be. It is best to try and surprise yourself in these circumstances, adjusting the angles of the mirror, looking up at the ceiling la-di-da, then quickly at your reflection, before you have a chance to think, sneaking up on your profile or your three-quarter face, like a stranger on the street. I always made sure to replace everything exactly as it had been.

I wish I had just an ounce of her neatness because I lose everything I touch. I never remember where my comb is or my hairbrush, or even my own pocketbook which I am constantly looking for. Buddy is more like my mother in this way. He hangs his own clothes up, his drawers are neat as a pin. He should have married her, har har har.

$\mathcal{I}$ went to the bank this afternoon and who did I see but old Eddie Shaw from high school. He is the only person I have run into so far and he says everybody is away on summer jobs. This is his real job, bank teller, so I am glad I didn't accidentally make fun of it. Eddie is a nice person. We were in the same science class, chemistry, which I flunked. He used to tell me these really dumb jokes which I thought were terribly funny. For example: What do Santa Claus and a mouse have in common? Answer: They both have beards except the mouse. I swear I laughed for a month at that, every time I thought of it I died laughing. Then in the twelfth grade Eddie used to call me up. I'd say, Hello? Hello? Hello? and he wouldn't say anything, then I'd hang up and two seconds later the phone would ring and it would be me, which he had recorded, saying, "Hello? Hello? Hello?"

Anyway, I went to the bank with the baby today. I made sure I had lipstick on and my hair looked nice and I was wearing an old pair of shorts I found in the closet from before. I looked okay in them, too. I didn't feel like a frump or an old fatty, the way I do in Hadley. I just feel thinner and prettier in Massachusetts.

At first he didn't recognize me.

"Hi, Ed," I said, handing a check to him. I had Madeline in my arms and she was trying to get down. She has just started walking and she wants to do it all the time. She takes off like a little human metronome, stiff-legged from side to side. But I didn't want her to go running around on the hard marble floor of the bank and so she was wiggling and squawking and I was trying to hold on to her. There is a thing babies can do where they just turn into this slippery tube that slides out of your grasp.

"Virginia?" Ed squinted at me, in mock surprise. "Is it really you?"

"It is really me, Eddie," I said. "Is it really you?" And I looked at his name plate which said EDWARD SHAW. "Edward?"

He nodded. "I heard you got married, Virginia," he said. "Is that your baby girl?" He still hadn't done anything with the check, he was just looking at me and then Maddie and then me again.

I nodded. "Sure is," I said proudly.

"Well," says Eddie, "she certainly is a little beauty, isn't she? What's her name?"

"Madeline," I said. "We call her Maddie for short." I smoothed her hair a little, getting it out of her eyes. Her bangs need cutting and her hair gets very messy in the back because it is curly.

"How would Madeline like a lollipop?" Eddie asked, fishing around in a drawer behind the counter. He handed me a red one. "Is it okay?" Maddie stopped wiggling and looked at him carefully. Her lips get very straight when she is thinking, it is the cutest thing. It all felt very strange, I have to say. All of a sudden Eddie was a bank teller and I was a mother. We were acting just right.

"Say thank you to Mr. Shaw," I told Madeline, who buried her face in my neck. I love it when she does this. "She's shy, Eddie," I said.

"Are you home for the summer?" Eddie asked, getting ready to count out my money. Fifty dollars for my mother.

"Just two weeks or so," I said. "We're just here while Maddie's daddy studies for his summer school exams." I always say "Maddie's daddy" instead of "my husband." I just can't make the words "my husband" come out of my mouth. "We're too much distraction, aren't we Maddie, especially these little cheeks," I said, and kissed her and kissed her. She would have protested except that would have meant taking the lollipop out of her mouth. You can usually kiss a baby all you want because they can't get away.

"Nobody much around," said Eddie. "Pretty quiet here." He handed me my money and another lollipop. "That one's for you," he said with a wink.

"Eddie, you look wonderful in a bank!" I said, right out of nowhere. I just felt happy. Here he was and here I was and we were both acting so nice to each other, the way life is supposed to be. "I guess I never saw you before in a white shirt or a tie. You look so good!"

Eddie blushed. I could see it happening behind his face, like somebody was pouring Pepto-Bismol in the top of his head and it filled up his neck and finally went up behind his face brimming at his hairline. Eddie is pale, like Chick. Blushes are so noticeable.

"Count your money, Virginia," he instructed me, suddenly very businesslike. "Never leave a teller's window without counting your money. First thing you need to know in this line of work."

"Perfect," I said. "Fifty dollars exactly. I love the smell of it," I said, taking a sniff. "New money smells exactly like a box of crayons."

"I never noticed that," said Eddie.

I smiled at him and then I put the money in my pocketbook. "Well, I hope I'll see you around," I said but

I didn't go rushing off. It was so nice to see him I hated to leave.

"How about I call you sometime?" asked Eddie. "Go out for a bite. Always wanted to go out with a married woman!"

"Well," I said, "that sounds very nice, Eddie. Sure. I'm sure that would be all right."

"Good. Then I'll give you a call."

On the way home from the bank I convinced Madeline to ride in her stroller by letting her hold a head of lettuce which we bought from Stanley's Superette. There were a few bunches of tourists in town, and I loved looking as if I belonged here, which I certainly did with a baby in a stroller who was holding groceries. But I found myself pushing Maddie down the street having terrible thoughts such as what would it be like to be married to Eddie? What kind of father would he be? And this is worst, what would it be like to kiss Eddie Shaw? I felt it would not be right to go out for a hamburger with him when and if he ever did call. I know it's wrong to imagine doing something with another person when you don't do it with your own husband.

At nine-thirty the phone rang and it was Eddie. I was already in my nightgown. I suppose for Eddie being an unmarried person without a small child the night was still young. I didn't know who he was dating if anybody. He asked me out for supper and I said yes, because what excuse could I make? We decided to eat at the Flying Clam next Thursday at seven-thirty. He said he'd pick me up. I didn't mention this to my mother or father as I didn't know what they would think. I found myself wondering what he was wearing when he called. How ridiculous.

"Who was that?" asked my daddy after I hung up the phone.

"Oh, that was just nobody," I said, and he didn't pursue it. I love my daddy.

That night I lay in bed and all I could think of was Eddie. I have to admit that I once did kiss Eddie at a party. He was going out with Yolanda, but we found ourselves in the kitchen by the icebox with the lights out and I let him kiss me. It was so nice I still remember it. Of course Eddie wouldn't recall since he was drunk at the time but I remember everything very clearly. He didn't try to feel me up, he was a gentleman. I have kissed a lot of boys. It was by far my favorite thing to do in the world, sit in their cars in the front seat and make out. I usually wore fairly tight sweaters. A lot of boys asked me out because they hoped I might be wild. Lots of ministers' daughters get wild. I wasn't crazy, but I did like to steam up the old windows, I have to say.

• • •

$\mathcal{B}$uddy told me once that if I hadn't gone out with him the first time he asked he would never have asked me again. God. I said, Really? Even if I'd had a doctor's appointment? Even if my father and mother had planned to come for a visit? He said he never asked a girl out twice. If she wasn't interested, he wasn't interested.

$\mathcal{I}$t has rained and blown two days in a row. Maddie and I take the umbrella and walk to the beach and look at the water. It is so exciting when the waves get huge and ragged like this, and you can hear the roar from downtown. It is scary, too, because the water is so dangerous you're afraid you might go crazy and run right into it. The hardest thing is to stand still and watch the huge waves come rolling in so heavy and you can't take your eyes off them at the same moment you think you'd better run away. It's hardest just to stand still, but I do, hanging on to Maddie for dear life.

I am waiting for the right moment to tell my parents I am invited to eat supper tonight with Eddie down at the Flying Clam. I'm not sure if they will approve and what with one thing and another I have left it until the last minute. I have given Maddie her supper and it is after seven o'clock, nearly her bedtime, and I put her in her little nightgown and plop her on my daddy's lap and say, "I think I'll take a little walk, is that okay with you?" My parents look at me blankly. Well, not blankly, they look all blinking-eyed as if they were fish and somebody has begun rudely tapping the aquarium.

"At this hour of the evening?" My mother looks suspicious. "Wherever would you go at this hour, Virginia?" she asks in that awful rubbery voice she gets.

"Well, actually, an old friend asked me if I'd like to meet him at the Flying Clam for a bite. Is it okay?"

"What friend is this, Virginia?" she says. "I thought you said you had no friends here." Well I did say that, because there hasn't been anyone to call up. Not even Elinor, who has been in New York City buying her damn trousseau, as my mother likes to point out.

"Well, actually, with my friend Eddie Shaw who works down at the bank now. Remember Eddie? He was really good in chemistry." I don't know what to say. I feel so ridiculous asking for permission but really I don't think I should go without making sure it is all right with them. But just asking makes me feel guilty, as if I have something wrong in mind. There is no way to do this and feel like a normal person.

"Run along," says my daddy, the sweetest man in the world. He has not been noticing my mother's face because of Maddie sitting on his lap. "Go have a good time. We'll get the baby to bed. Don't worry. Run along."

"Well, I guess it's decided then," says my mother, slapping her magazine hard against the arm of her chair. "Why bother to ask in the first place?" But I am halfway across the room headed toward the door.

"Oh thanks, I won't be late."

Maddie doesn't even notice me leave. She never minds anything if she is with her Pop-Pop. Once outside I put on my lipstick and a little rouge. I also take my hair down from the barrette and let some of it fall in my face. The Flying Clam is twelve blocks from here and nobody asked me how I am getting downtown. But there's Eddie waiting at the end of our driveway in his little red car and I just climb in. "Oh, this is so nice of you," I say, "to pick me up and everything."

Eddie looks at me. "Where's the kid?" he asks. He looks disappointed.

"Oh," I say, although my feelings are hurt, "my parents love to watch her."

"Well, hop in," says Eddie, and I do. "You mind the radio?" he asks, which is polite of him.

"I love the radio," I tell him. It is already on and Eddie turns it up.

When I was pregnant I stopped listening to rock 'n' roll and tuned in to the music of the big bands which I thought more suitable to a person who was having a baby. I learned all the words to everything, "Sleepy Time Gal" and "Begin the Beguine" not to mention "Stars Fell on Alabama." But I love Elvis Presley and I love Buddy Holly and I love Carl Perkins and I love the Midnights and Eddie's car radio is tuned to WBIG, and they're playing "Annie had a baby, can't work no more," which I have always thought secretly was my song, although I certainly wasn't like Annie, who-ever she might be, I certainly wasn't doing it all the time as I assume she was. But I love the song and I start singing along under my breath because this song makes it feel sexy to be knocked up, so to speak. That's what is so good about rock 'n' roll. It can make you feel sexy in any situation, even the worst ones. I don't know how. It also makes you feel somewhat powerful. Anyway, Eddie is driving along and then it is Elvis and my heart just about pounds out of my body. I can't help it, I am just feeling good all of a sudden. I haven't felt this way in so long. I am already won-dering if Eddie is thinking about kissing me. I know I shouldn't be thinking such things. But I can't just sweep out my brain and start with a whole different set of thoughts, can I? Not that I would ever actually kiss him. Eddie keeps his eyes on the road, but he nods his head to the music and neither of us say anything until we get to the restaurant.

I am wearing an old pair of jeans and I know I look good but nobody could accuse me of getting dressed up. I also have on my red sweater which is very flattering despite everything and a green jacket on top of that so I don't have to look sexy unless I want to, or unless I get too hot and just have to take the jacket off. I can't help wanting to feel this certain kind of power I have in certain clothes. Even if I don't do anything with it, which I certainly would not, it is nice to think I had at least a little power left. Even though I know it is ridiculous. Because after all, look where it got me. Har har.

We get to the Flying Clam and stand like adults behind the Please Wait to be Seated sign, which proves we are older since there were three empty booths and if we were in high school we'd have just sat in one. The hostess shows us to our booth and we sit down and Eddie tucks his napkin in his belt and hands me the menu. He is still wearing his work clothes, a white shirt and a dark necktie and a jacket. "We remind me of something," I say when I am all settled in the nice squashy red booth.

"What?" Eddie takes a sip of water.

"Oh, I don't know. A movie."

"Sad movie? American movie?"

"I don't know exactly."

Then the waitress comes and holds her little pad and pencil at the ready.

Eddie studies the menu for two seconds and then orders the hamburger platter with a side of onion rings and I order black coffee and fried clams.

"Strips or bellies?" asks the waitress, whom I don't recognize. She isn't Marie. Marie knows I always order bellies but I can't stand to say the word.

"She'll have the bellies," said Eddie. Everybody knew this foible of mine and the fact that Eddie remembered made me want to hug him.

"Oh, thanks, Eddie," I say, "for remembering."

"What's to forget, Virginia? The only girl on the eastern seaboard who'd order fried clam tummies." And we begin laughing only I can't stop. Tears are streaming down my cheeks. Eddie reaches over and grabs my wrist. "You okay?"

"Oh, yes," I say, but I keep laughing. "Oh yes," and laugh some more. "I just can't stop when I get started sometimes." Eddie lets me stop by myself. He tears some of his napkin into little pieces and rolls them in balls and makes faces on the table. Eddie was always making art as I recall. Then our food comes.

"How is it to work in a bank?" I ask him.

"It's steady," said Eddie. "Steady work. Pay's not too good but it's regular and there is plenty of room for advancement. You just have to mind your p's and q's." Well, I feel sorry for Eddie having to mind his p's and q's since he is such a funny boy but he looks uncomfortable when I say so.

"Do you still make those funny phone calls?" I ask him.

"No," he says. "I got over that."

"It was so imaginative, what you used to do," I say. "It used to drive me crazy that you fooled me every time.

'Hello? Hello?' It was so funny, Eddie. I thought you should go into radio."

"Well," says Eddie, "it's nice of you to say. But the bank is good enough for me. I don't mind the hours, either," he says.

"Remember the beach parties?" I say. "Remember the bonfires and everything? I think about them all the time," I say. I smile and take off my jacket as it is warm inside. This leaves me in my red sweater.

"Yolanda works over at the BonBon," says Eddie quickly, shaking pepper all over everything. "She said to say hello and all that," he says. "We've been going along pretty steady for coming up on three years now. She's managing the place. Yolanda has a head for business, turns out. Lucky for me, I think," he says.

"Really? That's wonderful," and I squeeze a little lemon on the rest of my clams. "It is so wonderful to have a child, Eddie," I say, changing the subject completely. Whenever I'm stuck for conversation I use Maddie. It's like having this wonderful prop you can just ad lib away about. "It is so satisfying to be a mother," I say. "You know, to have brought a new life into being." I am chowing down the clams. "She's almost a year old now."

"Where are you going to be living?" he asks.

"Well, we're sort of living where Buddy grew up for the summer," I say. "Then we will go back to Pittsburgh so he can finish school. Then I don't know where." And I really don't. I guess I never thought about this before. We will actually have to live somewhere. This is kind of scary and my mind goes blank for a second. "I think Buddy might want to travel around the country," I say. "I think he may have wanderlust. At least I hope so. It's funny, we don't know everything about each other yet, of course. There is so much to discover. I think he is going to be a teacher of some sort," I add and then I push a little piece of clam around in the tartar sauce. I hope Eddie doesn't notice I am sounding like such an idiot.

"What's it like being married?" asks Eddie, holding a forkful of onion rings. "If you don't mind such a personal question." He sticks them in his mouth and wipes his chin with his napkin shreds. Then he smiles at me. Eddie is really such a nice person.

"I don't exactly know how to describe it," I say. "I can't put it into words exactly."

It turns out Eddie is thinking of asking Yolanda to marry him and he really does want to know what it is like. He goes on and on about her, how wonderful this and how wonderful that, how beautiful and talented she is and how excellently she sews. She made him his jacket, even. "God," I said, "the lapels and everything?" Eddie nodded proudly.

"She is such a good girl," he says, lowering his voice,

making sure that I know what he means by that. It doesn't mean just that she lives at home with her crippled mother. It means she is still a virgin. Well, big deal. I get kind of tired of all this. After all, Yolanda is just an ordinary regular person, she is not like a goddess on high. I know Yolanda slightly myself and she has extremely small ears. A sign of selfishness, but I do not inform Eddie of this fact.

To be honest, I guess part of me was hoping Eddie was harboring some hidden huge love for me, and that he would betray a desire to carry me off somewhere, like the prince in a fairy tale. "Virginia, you have always been my one true love and I want you to drop everything and run away with me to a desert island with the baby." Not that I could ever do such a thing. Also, I am far from being a princess or any other worthy person. I don't know what is wrong with me, but I could never smile at anyone the way Snow White smiles at those dwarves. I'd be thinking, Why does he have hair growing out of his ears? or some such terrible thing. This is part of not being a true Christian, but there is nothing I can do about it.

When Eddie drops me home he shakes my hand and tells me to give a kiss to the little girl. He can't even remember her name. I feel so strange. The whole thing was really just to see how marriage agreed with me so he could decide whether to pop the question or not. I feel sort of mean when I get out of the car. "I don't know, Eddie," I say, "to tell you the truth. Maybe you ought to hang on to it yourself a while longer," and I huff up the path to the porch. I don't know what got into me. I should never have said such a horrible thing. I just get lonelier and lonelier when I think of other people being happy. I am a vicious person and there is nothing I can do about it.

$\mathcal{D}$id Buddy call?" I only asked once so far. My mother frowned and shook her head and my daddy looked worried. "Oh, good," I said immediately. It was better to pretend we had planned it that way. "Well," I said, "that's good. Then's he's following our plan. We decided it would make us miss each other too much to talk on the phone. I'm glad he's sticking to his side of the bargain. It was all my idea," I added. "We haven't really been separated for the last twenty months or so. We're very dependent on each other." This is such a lie. The thing is I am waiting to see how long it takes him to call. I think he should call first. I am not calling until he calls us first.

Then when I went to bed I was remembering last winter while Buddy was at school and how nice it was when he came home at night to our tiny half-painted apartment and he studied and I read a book and Maddie was fast asleep. We didn't talk much then either, but at least it was cozy. Most nights Buddy and I tickled feet. It is not actual tickling, it is more like rubbing. You put the other person's foot in your lap and you put your foot in his, and then you start by smoothing the ankle bones, maybe, or the top of the foot (the bottom is too ticklish to start with), then you can eventually do the whole thing. And feet are not so bad as you might think. They are normally nice and warm and dry when exposed to the air. But it feels good and soothing and you stay up much later than if you're not doing feet. You don't really feel like going to bed. You don't have to talk to the other person except now and then you say, "Tickle," when they've drifted off, or "You've stopped tickling," and give your foot a shake. I could have mentioned to Eddie about tickling. Except it doesn't last.

My mother is out of bed now and she sits in the living room for a couple of hours every afternoon. I like to bring her toast and tea. She likes cinnamon toast. When I do this I feel like the ladies in the magazine ads who are opening their iceboxes and smiling out at you, saying, Here I am and here is the icebox full of good food. The only thing missing is the little apron with cherries all over and a pair of pumps which I never wear. Anyway, I could never cook in high heels. I like to be barefoot in the house. My mother however always wears not just shoes but stockings too. And her bathrobes are silky quilted pale blues and pinks. She keeps a handkerchief tucked up her sleeve and she has never chewed gum in her entire life. My mother murmurs,

"Thank you, Virginia dear," when I bring her the treats on a tray. I murmur, "Oh you're so welcome, Mother."

At moments like this it is impossible for me to believe either one of us has ever seen a human penis.

Elinor is back and I'm waiting at the beach for her to show up. She makes me laugh my head off and it will be nice to see her. I told her I'd gone out with Eddie and I could almost hear her eyebrows go up over the phone. "Oh-ho," said Elinor. She knows we had our little kiss that time. She knows I liked Eddie. "Elinor," I said, "don't be ridiculous. Besides, he's marrying Yolanda." I had to whisper this because my mother was in the other room and her ears are so good. "That never stopped anyone I know of," said Elinor. She is so cynical when it comes to men.

Elinor was really a wild and fast girl and where I might make out with a couple of boys Elinor was actually doing the deed, and had been since she was fourteen years old when she suddenly sprouted big bosoms. El is the person who told me that a girl's chest gets bigger the first time a boy touches it. I said I bet a boy made that one up and she said it had happened to her so it was a fact. Sometimes I felt shy around Elinor even though we were friends, because she was really sophisticated. El's parents are rich, her daddy owns a Coca-Cola bottling plant somewhere down south. That is why she has a fourteen-karat gold toothpick, among other things. But of course I am a mother now, which makes us sort of more equal. I don't know exactly why she started to like me, except one time when Barry was bothering her for a date I happened to be sitting at the next table. Barry didn't see why Elinor wouldn't go out with him since she was such an easy lay, as he put it. I don't know what got into me but I walked over to him and I said, "Stuff it up your ass." I shocked myself but it felt good. Elinor and I started eating our lunch together. Not that she needed me. Elinor is very self-sufficient.

"Hey, Virginia!" I hear this loud shout and there she is running toward me. El is a very beautiful girl, there are no two ways about it. You can't help noticing her. She has a tiny space between her two front teeth which means lucky in love or lucky in cards, and she has that silky blond hair that looks like it's made out of water maybe, rushing down her scalp. I can't describe it. If you walk around with El you could be totally naked and nobody would look at you. But with El you don't get jealous, you don't feel bad, because she pays attention when she's with you and that feels so nice. She is genuinely interested in the people she considers her friends. I think this is unusual in a beautiful girl.

"Just look at this child!" exclaims Elinor, zeroing in on Madeline. I can smell her perfume. Elinor wears perfume even to the beach. "Virginia, she's just a little beauty! Really! Look at those eyes! Look at those curls. Oh, you're a little devil, aren't you, sweetheart," and Elinor takes Maddie's hand and leans over to give it a kiss. Madeline has such a solemn look on her face. This is how Maddie sometimes is with strangers: she waits to see what they will do next. El keeps Maddie's hand in hers and I notice her great big ring.

"So how's the little wifey!" says El, and she gives me a one-armed hug and kisses me on both cheeks. She learned this in Europe and it always impresses my mother. "God, I'm sorry my mother called your mother. I gave her hell about it after." That is another difference between El and me. I could not imagine saying "gave my mother hell" about anything on this earth.

"You mean the letter? Oh, that blew over," I said. "And I'm fine, I guess."

"You guess? You mean you're not blissful? What a surprise." Elinor is very cynical about the institution of marriage. Her mother has been married three times. Now she is taking off her blouse and unzipping her shorts and if there were anybody else on the beach at this hour they would be staring as El is wearing a very small bathing suit which should be outlawed here.

"What about you?" I ask, trying not to look as she stuffs one of her breasts into the teeny little top piece. "Is that

crocheted, El?" I can't help asking. "Won't that come apart
in the water?"

"Oh, I certainly hope so," says El. "I most certainly hope
so." That is the kind of wonderful girl she is. She loves to
shock. It is never boring around her. She looks at Maddie,
who is sitting on my lap. "Honestly, Virginia, how did you
ever do it?"

"What? Have a baby?"

"It scares me to death to think of all those hours of suf-
fering." Elinor shudders delicately. "I'm so impressed with
you I can't begin to say it. The throes of labor. God. Was it
as bad as they say? Did you scream obscenities at your
adorable husband?"

"Well, it was fairly bad. I didn't scream at all. Buddy
wasn't around anyway. He thought it would take longer
and he went out to grab a sandwich."

Elinor frowns. "That doesn't sound very sportsmanlike."

"It wasn't his fault. Usually it takes longer."

"I think I'll arrange to have someone else bear my children for me." Elinor is just standing there looking at me.
"Maybe you could make me one of those." And she points
at Maddie.

"So how are you?" I ask. "When's the big day?"

"The big day?" Elinor looks puzzled. "Oh, that." She
spreads a large royal blue towel on the sand and sits down
on it. "Well, at least I will certainly not be going back to

college. A ghastly experience. My roommate nailed a string from one end of the room to the other and then do you know what she did? She cleaned her comb on it. Can you imagine? How could I stay in a charnel house like that? I came home for spring vacation and just never looked back."

"What did your parents say?"

"What could they do? Put me in chains? There was nothing they could say. They sent me to Europe and I came home with an engagement ring." She holds up her left hand.

"Yikes," I say to be polite. "Wowee."

"Tasteless, I know, but I'm not complaining." El flashes me a smile. I have been putting suntan lotion on Maddie's arms and legs and now I put her sun hat on her. We have brought a pail and a big spoon and Maddie is happily digging away. It is one of those nice mornings where the sun is hot but the breeze is still cool. I love how the sun glitters off the water. Today the ocean has big swollen waves, and the color is more like a dark blue. I don't always swim when the water is this dark, but I love to look at it. There aren't many people on the beach this early in the morning. Generally the beach fills up by one o'clock. Today it's just me and Madeline and El, and a few other mothers with kids down closer to the water. We like to lie up in the dunes for privacy. A couple of boys are sitting on the lifeguard chair with the lifeguard. One of them has noticed us, and I can see him standing on his hands on the lifeguard seat. Boys can be so ridiculous, but they are so transparent sometimes it is kind of touching. They can't help themselves. It is Elinor. She heats them up like a skillet even at this distance.

Elinor's favorite food is jelly beans and she has a little bag of them that she carries with her everywhere. Now she puts a blue one in her belly button and lies down. "Pretty cute, huh," says El and closes her eyes. "God, make me brown," says El. "Make me into a goddess." Well, that's embarrassing since she already is somewhat of a goddess. Maddie comes crawling over and reaches carefully into El's belly button for the jelly bean. And we all three laugh, Maddie too, with those funny giggles that erupt from her in little spurts. I take away the jelly bean which is slippery with suntan oil and give her a zwieback from our bag but Maddie wants the candy. "Like it, like it!" she sobs and El fishes her out a clean one from her bag. "Now you chew this very carefully, Madeline," says Elinor. "No choking allowed on this beach."

I love El, I can't help it. I just do. She is so funny and so generous and she always makes me feel better about everything. "Sit down," she orders, patting her towel and turning over on her stomach. "Put this stuff on my back." She shoves a bottle of Coppertone into my hand. I squeeze some out and do her back. It is strange but since I was married I haven't touched another human being except Madeline, not even Buddy in so long. It gives me such a weird feeling, there is El's warm nice back and right next to her is Maddie's, which is so little. It gives me big/little. That's where you feel odd because something is way out of proportion, like an aspirin next to a pillow. It is a physical sensation and uncomfortable, the inside of you wants to get out and run away is the only way I can describe it. It is not something I enjoy in the slightest. Most people just stare at you when you describe it but Elinor gets the same thing. It is always interesting when you have weird things in common to cement a friendship. "This is giving me big/little, El," I said. "You and Madeline."

"Just get it over with and stop complaining," said El, her face in the towel.

The other thing we have in common is that we were both the new girls here three years ago. Elinor had moved from Kentucky (although she hasn't got a southern accent) and I had moved from Missouri. We had both been to a million schools. "As usual, the new girl," Elinor said. "You too?" She carried rubbers in her pocketbook. "You never know," she had said, and shocked the world. We were also the best dancers in the school. "Where did you learn that?" she asked me when she saw me bop. "I taught myself," I told her, "listening to Carl Perkins's 'Blue Suede Shoes.'" She thought they only knew how to do it down south, but I taught myself in my bedroom all one winter by playing

"Blue Suede Shoes" over and over and practicing the foot movements until I got good. I did it to impress Brady Boggs, the baddest boy in the world, and then when he saw me he said I danced too dirty so I wound up dancing by myself while everybody watched. They treated me with new respect after that.

Later on, after we have lain around for a while sopping up the rays as El calls the sun, she goes into her bag and digs up a picture of the count. His name is Reynardo Pellagrini. He doesn't even look Italian, he looks sort of mousey and small and he is wearing a suit that looks too big for him. There she is hanging on his arm. In the background is a castle and some mountains. It looks like a painting.

"He's mad for me," says El.

"God, El," I say. I can't think of anything else to say. "He looks really cute," I make myself say. "God, a real count."

"You lie," says Elinor. "He is not cute. But he's smart and he's rich, and he is a count. And they really know how to treat a woman in Europe." Elinor lies on her back now. She puts a gold toothpick between her two front teeth and leaves it there. She got this for her birthday two years ago. A solid gold toothpick. She can do all sorts of tricks with it in her mouth, put it in sideways, pretend to swallow it, puff on it like a teeny cigar (which also gives me big/little), all the while making Groucho Marx faces. She can really make you laugh.

"I can't believe you're getting married, El, after all that talk."

"Engaged is not married," said El. "And it's going to be a long engagement. It just gets me out of this boring place and off to sunny Italy. I can live with that. The thing is," says Elinor, out of the clear blue sky, "after I'm sleeping with someone awhile I want them to brush every single tooth a thousand times before I let them touch me. It's awful when you know what they've been eating."

"Oh, I know," I say, but in fact I can't imagine telling Buddy to go brush his teeth. I can't imagine asking Buddy to do anything. At least not anymore. Not now that we know each other a little better and it turns out that we are actually strangers.

"And the thing is," El goes on, "they look so dumb."

"How do you mean?" I am sitting up now. "How do you mean dumb?"

"When they're doing it. They look so dumb. Like dogs. Or bears."

"You mean because they're on their knees?"

"Unless they have perfect bodies." And she pats her own flat abdomen. Elinor is completely brown already all over.

"You mean about their stomachs hanging down?" I want to laugh so badly. I am loving this conversation.

"Yeah. On *you*," which makes me laugh. "Did you ever go to one of those hotels that has a mirror on the ceiling?"

I shake my head. "No," I said. "Not yet."

"That's enough to turn you off sex forever. They look like frogs!"

"El!" I shriek.

"Big fat frogs."

"Stop, El," I say, "I can't stand it." So she stops and waits until I am done laughing. Then when I am calmed down she starts again. Once she gets started you can't stop her. It is a matter of pride with Elinor to see how long she can keep you laughing.

"But the worst is when they have a tiny penis," she says seriously.

"Oh, I know," I say. I try to sound as if I've seen millions of penises.

"When I first saw Reynardo's I wanted to say, Hey, honey, I'm sorry but I just can't *work* with this."

"Oh, El," I said, and my stomach was starting to ache from laughing, "stop it. It hurts me to laugh so hard."

I had forgotten how much better El makes me feel. Whatever I feel guilty about she doesn't feel guilty about at all. It is so refreshing. I don't think she loves Reynardo at all. She just wants a completely different life, that's all. We lie there for a while in the dunes and Maddie throws tiny fistfuls of sand until we tell her to stop and then she fills up Elinor's belly button with sand and the waves make their nice nervous sound and all the worrying just drains out of me. Then Elinor sits up and her top falls off.

"El!" I say, pointing and looking away.

"Oh, who cares. In Europe this is de rigueur." But she lazily ties herself together again. "Listen," she says. "If you get miserable down there in the bowels of the earth"—this is how she refers to New Jersey—"drop me a line. I'll send you two plane tickets, for you and the baby. Come live with me in a villa in southern Italy. We'll have a ball."

"Thanks, El," I say, and I know she means it. I could of course never do any such thing. It's not like an actual choice. I look over at Maddie, who has gathered a feather and a whole bunch of pebbles, and she is stirring everything very seriously in her little pail. My life has already been decided and all I have to do is live it out.

"Last one in's a rotten egg," says Elinor, suddenly getting to her feet.

I pick Maddie up and we walk down to the water. This is a blue flag day meaning be careful, but Elinor just goes plowing in anyway and rides a wave that washes her up at our feet and when she sits up I see she's lost her bathing suit.

"Top and bottom," she shrieks, and then she just lies there in the sand laughing with the water swirling around her.

"I'll get you a towel, El, don't worry, just stay put," I say, as if she were bleeding to death and needing a tourniquet. But she isn't worried. El just does not care. She just has no shame whatsoever. There are half a dozen people trying not to stare while she stands up and heads back into the waves. I try not to stare too, but it is impossible not to look at Elinor naked and wet and brown all over walking casually as you please back into the water. Her hair is wet and the color of foam and her back is so long and her behind has those two dimples and her legs are practically up to her collarbone. God. I can't not look at Elinor and I hear a few whistles from the lifeguard chair and some dirty talk which just makes me so mad. How can they talk like that? Elinor is beautiful, that's all, you just have to be in awe of her. She is not something to be pawed over by two beer guzzlers. They should be forbidden even to have an opinion about her. But I race back up the beach with Maddie and back down again as fast as I can carrying her big blue towel.

"Hey!" I am yelling and waving the towel.

But she doesn't come out right away. She swims around another couple of minutes in spite of there being other people in the water now, all of them pretending not to look. Now and then she does a surface dive and you can see her behind naked as a jaybird and then when she comes up you can see her breasts. It is terribly embarrassing but also kind of lovely, I have to say. She looks wild and beautiful, and it looks like so much fun. She waves to me, yelling, "Come on in! I'm naked and you've got all your clothes on! Come on in! What a crazy sight! One girl starkers and the other girl dressed!" Well, she does not realize I have Madeline to think about and can't just go tearing into the surf leaving my baby girl on the sand. So I feel somewhat angry although it all fades when she gets out. "Oh," she says, as I hold the towel around her. "Oh that was glorious," and she shakes her head just like a dog and water sprays out all over me and Maddie. "Thanks, Virginia," she says. We walk back up to our blanket and El is so beautiful and I feel like a sad little thing made of tin. Then I notice up in the parking lot a cop has gotten out of a car with all its red lights flashing.

"Don't look now," I say.

"Oh for God's sake. What's he going to do? Give me a ticket for skinny-dipping?" Elinor honestly does not care what anybody thinks. It is so admirable. She also speaks three languages, French, Italian, and English. I guess she could do anything she wanted to and get away with it.

"Elinor, I mean it, he is coming over. Keep your towel on. Just tell him you lost your suit and went back in the water to hide," I say.

Here he comes, this sort of overweight cop wearing a gun, for God sakes, and he chugs along the sand. He is red in the face and there is something in the corner of one eye he needs to wipe off. "See here, young lady," he begins but Elinor interrupts immediately.

"Qu'est-ce que c'est?" she asks, looking at me. *"Qu'est-ce que cet homme ici fait? Comme il est laid,"* she says, wrinkling her nose.

The policeman looks at me. "Your friend here speak English?"

"Oh, officer," I say, "her suit came off in the water. She was just hiding out there."

"O pauvre moi," says Elinor, in a piteous voice. *"Avez pitié sur pauvre petite moi."* I think that is a bit much but it has the desired effect because he puts his big pad back in his pocket.

"Well, I'll let her off with just a warning this time," he says. "Tell her we don't tolerate nudity on our beaches over here. Not in the U. S. of A. This isn't a Brigitte Bardot movie over here."

"No," I say, "it certainly isn't. No. I'll explain it to her. Thank you." I'm much too nervous to laugh.

"Brigitte Bardot? *Vous avez vu* And God Created Womans?" Elinor has that maniacal look in her eyes and she takes a step toward the cop. *"Vous avez vu cette femme magnifique?"* With every word Elinor takes another step closer and the cop takes another step back.

"Non, non," he says, looking at me as if for protection. His eyes are rolling like a calf about to be slaughtered. "Tell

her *non non.*" He has his arm out now, as if to fend her off.
I know he is afraid she is going to drop her towel because I
am afraid of it too. He finally turns and scrambles back up
the beach with as much dignity as he can muster.

"You tell her," he calls over his shoulder. "Tell her now."

"I'll tell her everything you said," I yell. Then I look at El.
"You took a big chance. Suppose he had spoken French?"

"Then I'd have switched to Italian," she says.

With Elinor they always bite off more than they can
chew. That's why I love her.

"Well, that's that," she says. "No more swimming for
your old aunt El today," and she pats Maddie's tummy. She
gets into her clothes and lies down on her towel again.
"You want to hear a good joke?"

"Sure," I say.

"Well, there's this old Italian man named Luigi and he's
engaged to marry this young girl but she doesn't want to
marry him and she keeps putting him off."

"Why is she engaged to him?" I interrupt.

"You have such a literal mind, Virginia. She's engaged to
him that's all. And anyway, her mother is helping her think
of impossible things to ask for. 'Tell him you can't marry
him until he buys you a thousand mink coats.' But unfortu-
nately he keeps coming up with everything she asks for.
The sky's the limit type of thing. 'A thousand mink coats?
Hey,' he says. 'You lika Luigi, Luigi lika you, Luigi buya da

coats.' 'A castle in Spain? A Rolls-Royce? A hundred Arabian horses?' Her mother comes up with one impossible thing after another and every time he says, 'Hey. You lika Luigi, Luigi lika you, Luigi buy da horses.' Finally the mother has a brainstorm. 'Tell him you can't marry him unless he has a fifteen-inch penis.' So the girl goes back and says, 'I can't marry you unless you have a fifteen-inch penis.' Luigi doesn't say anything at first and the girl thinks, Oh boy, I'm out of this. And then he shrugs, 'Hey. You lika Luigi, Luigi lika you, Luigi cut offa two inches!'"

Elinor looks at me to see if I think it's funny, which I do. It is funny.

"Did Reynardo cut offa two inches?" I ask.

"Don't be silly. He was born that way," she laughs. "I was flunking out," Elinor says suddenly. "I hadn't done two licks of work the whole time. I just could not make myself open a book." I wasn't sure what to say to that so I didn't say anything.

She is so outspoken. Except when she asks how Buddy is in the sex department. "How's your Prince Charming in the sack?" is the way she puts it, and I say, "Oh, he is fine," and when I don't elaborate she knows enough to let the subject drop. I am glad El has tact. How can I tell her we don't do anything? Even though she has revealed herself to me in the sack department I would hate for her to feel sorry for me because I will never again feel the thrill of a boy's arms around me trying to cop a feel. I liked it so much better before, when you weren't supposed to do it. We lie there awhile each with our separate thoughts and then Elinor puts on her sunglasses and props herself on one elbow and asks me an interesting question.

"Why do they call it carnal knowledge? What's to know? Do you feel any smarter?"

I shake my head. "No," I say. "Mostly I feel like an idiot."

After a while we pack up. Madeline is getting hot and fussy and it is time for her nap. Elinor drives us home in her baby blue Cadillac and we have the top down and the radio blaring and I have to keep Maddie's hat from blowing off her head. Elinor asks me do I want to go to a dance over in Milford tomorrow night with her and a couple of friends. I would love to go but I certainly can't. I hate how much I want to go to the dance.

Buddy hates my dancing. He didn't even like it before we got married. He himself can't dance a step. He can sing, though, I'll say that for him. He can sing and he can play the guitar. He just doesn't do it anymore. I think I squashed all that in him. He certainly would never write me a song, of course. What would he say? "I had to get married, boohoohoo, I feel like a really sad elf, I had to get married, boohoohoo, I had to put my penis on the shelf."

Har har.

• • •

ℋow is Elinor?" asks my mother later. "Such a nice girl."

"Oh, she's fine. We had a great time at the beach."

"When is she leaving for Europe?" my mother wants to know.

"I forgot to ask."

"Oh, Virginia, surely you must have asked that." My mother is reading the *Atlantic Monthly* and can't be bothered to lift her eyes from the page. This means she is really interested.

"No, really. I forgot. She showed me a picture of her husband-to-be," I say and then I just wait. Tick, tick, tick. That's the only kind of power you have over my mother, when you know she's dying to know something and hates to ask. I think it makes her feel like a poor person to ask a question that she really wants to know the answer to. It makes her feel like a beggar. So I make her be a beggar sometimes, whenever I can, if I'm in a bad mood. If I'm feeling mean.

"Oh, really?" is all she lets herself say at first. I nod and pick up a magazine myself. *Life* magazine with a picture of Elizabeth Taylor on the cover. I can tell it is killing her not to know but she lets several seconds drift by before she speaks. "And what does he look like?" She acts as if she doesn't really care but my mother does not ask questions she does not want to know the answer to. That is why she asks so few questions.

"Actually, he looked kind of old," I say. "I hate to burst your bubble but he wasn't wearing like a crest or anything and he looked as if he were going bald on top. He also looked short. No crown, either."

My mother gives me an angry look. "You did not as you call it 'burst my bubble.' I can't imagine what makes you think you can speak to me that way, Virginia," she says, in her freezing-cold voice. Miss Baked Alaska 1960. Mrs. Baked Alaska.

"Oh, Mother," I say. "It is just an expression, for God sakes."

"It is not an expression I care for. I am not in the habit of having illusions about life. At least certainly not anymore," and her voice breaks halfway through the sentence. God. Me, of course. So she goes to her room and I go into the bedroom and pick up Maddie who is waking up from her nap.

$\mathcal{I}$ gave my mother a stack of dinner plates with pictures of all the different college dorms on them for Xmas the year before I got pregnant. After they kicked me out my mother broke every plate in half in the kitchen sink and threw them in a box. She didn't say one word. She didn't even wear goggles to do it, she could have put an eye out. "Oh, Mother," I said, "we can just throw them out." She didn't even glance in my direction. That's how much she hated that place for kicking me out.

$\mathcal{I}$ have to say it is easier here without Buddy. I know that you rise to your feet when a grown-up enters the room even if you are lying on the sofa reading a book. That is the way you show respect to an elder and I always get up when my mother comes into a room. Buddy doesn't know this. We were here for two days at Christmas and it was terrible. I could see my mother giving him such a look when she came into the living room and he kept sitting there reading a book or playing with the baby or just staring dumbly into space. Buddy really doesn't have bad manners. He has different manners. I would like to explain this to my mother but she has already made up her mind and her face is a closed door, so to speak. If I bring up his name there is the same little frozen look it gets. She can't help it. She can't pretend with her expressions. She can pretend with words sometimes. "Oh, Virginia, I meant no such thing!" she might say if I say, "You said you hated his name." She'll say, "I said nothing of the kind." "Doesn't that young man have a real name?" is what she said when I first brought him home. That sounds to me like "I hate his damn name." But she gets angry if I insist, as if I am making the whole thing up.

$\mathcal{I}$ called Buddy but there was no answer. I wanted to tell him his daughter is now saying the word "Peas!" I thought he might like it for a joke. She means "please" of course, but it sounds like "peas," and maybe he would think that was funny since she really does not care for the vegetable as he well knows. I tried twice but there was no answer. Even late at night, which worried me somewhat. But I felt strangely distant from it too. Like if I am not sleeping in the little white house where he is supposed to be I'm not sure I can care too much where he is. It seems kind of hazy at a distance. Plus thank goodness I don't lie here wishing he would die in a flaming car wreck. I just lie here thinking, Where is my life? I am homesick for my life. But I have a feeling that is part of growing up so there is nothing to be done about it.

Daddy gave me a serious talk in the kitchen. I don't know why. He was making himself a cup of coffee and he asked did I want to know the secret of a happy marriage? I said, "Oh yes, Daddy, do tell me." We have never talked like this before, like one grown-up to another, and it was very strange for me. I felt like I was onstage and did not know what my lines could possibly be. Then he said the secret is one person has to love the other person more than that person is loved. One person has to be willing to give up more than the other person is willing to give up. And you can never tell the other person, either. You just do it quietly. He blushed when he said this. I did not dare ask him which person he was.

And as far as me and Buddy go, it would have to be me in that role and I do not think I feel quite that way myself. I suppose that at heart I have not an ounce of the true Christian in me. In this regard I am just like my mother.

There are many ways in which I resemble my mother. I take pride in speaking a proper English sentence. I know many poems by heart. My mother believes the brain is a muscle and you should exercise it. A couple of years ago she memorized one Wordsworth sonnet a week which means quite a few of them are in her repertoire. At the drop of a hat she might recite one. The one that always comes to her mind is "Getting and spending we lay waste our powers, nothing we see in nature that is ours." She will say this in all kinds of ways for a joke: "Cooking and eating we lay waste our powers," or "Watching TV we lay waste our powers," except my mother doesn't say "TV," she says "television." She believes in reading. She read me every Oz book in the world when I was a little girl and once she asked me if I would like to go to Oz and I said yes I would. And then she says I said, "But the thing is, first we've got to get to Kansas." My mother says that all the time when it is appropriate. "But first we've got to get to Kansas" or "The thing is . . ." and then we all know what she means.

One of my big fights with Buddy was over his criticism

of my mother. I know she is moody, I don't deny that fact. But I don't think he is free to discuss her. He does not realize you don't just talk about her in an ordinary way with any Tom, Dick, or Harry sitting around the kitchen with a beer in your hand. My mother is not someone to bring up in casual conversation. She is not an ordinary run-of-the-mill person.

"Your mother is a snob," said Buddy, "and she is moody as hell." Well, what is so wrong with being a snob? That's what I want to know. Of course she is a snob. She has certain standards as do I. I threw a beer cap at him and he pretended to duck and hold his hands up in pretend fear. But he did quit bringing her up. What got him was the fact that she happens to keep her jelly jars on doilies inside the icebox and I do not see what is so wrong with that. If she wants to why shouldn't she? It's her house, isn't it? And if she does not care for certain kinds of language so what? She happens to hate the words "tossed salad." It sounds like something on a diner menu to her. If she asks somebody please not to refer to it as a tossed salad but simply as a salad what is so difficult about that? She was just being nice, that is what is so terrible. She was just trying to teach him something nicely. She does not believe in making plain things sound fancy. She also hates the words "pot-luck supper." And once she said the three saddest words in the English language were "covered candy dish."

Anyway, if anybody is going to get mad at my parents it is going to be me. I am the only one with the right.

Today my mother fell asleep in her chair in broad daylight. Her chin dropped down and her mouth just fell open. She looked like an entirely different person to me. She looked almost sweet. She looked old, too, which I did not expect and I could see many more gray hairs on top of her head, as if somebody had dumped an ashtray there. My mother would be furious if I compared her hair to cigarette ashes. My mother needs to be given a great deal of respect. But she looked so helpless asleep like that with her mouth open and these very tiny snores coming out of her. I could not believe a person such as my mother snored. It made me want to hug her, or pat her on the arm or something. I must have been just staring into her face because when she woke up and opened her eyes she saw I was looking right at her and she looked puzzled, not having her bearings quite, but I could not look away, I was glued to the spot as if she had found me out in a lie, but I smiled what I hoped was like a tender little smile, and then thank God she made the blank look come over her face. This is where all expression is removed and you can't tell any emotions are there at all. Then she closed her eyes and when she opened them again I was reading my book just as if nothing had happened. Which, of course, nothing had. But then she came over and actually put her hand on my head for two seconds.

"Would you like a cup of tea?" she asked. I could not believe my ears.

"Oh, yes, Mother," I said, jumping out of my chair. "I'll make it."

And we sat in the kitchen which was very nice, like old times, her and me at the table, both of us looking at our magazines and sipping our tea out of her grandma's little tiny cups which have handles so small you can't put any part of any finger through them. And she was telling me about William Wordsworth and his sister Dorothy and she recited "Westminster Bridge" but then she burst into tears over the line "Dear God! the very houses seem asleep; And all that mighty heart is lying still!"

The older my mother gets the harder it is for her to get through a poem in one piece, she tells me. "O Western Wind, when wilt thou blow" always makes her cry. I don't think my mother has told me this before. I don't know what to say. She is telling me something very important now and I hope I will know what to make of it. Every now and then she does this. She takes the lid off a little box for just one second, long enough for me to know there is something very important inside, and the clue is a line of poetry or perhaps the color red of a cloak in the piece of stained glass window she once saw depicting the four seasons "and winter's cloak was of such a ruby red that it caused me to weep." She doesn't say my name. She doesn't say, "It caused me to weep, Virginia," and then look at me. She is looking into space when she talks this way, and I just listen. I am a very good listener. I am listening for the secrets of life that I do not yet know.

$\mathcal{I}$ am a help to my parents. I do the cooking and the laundry, which is too heavy a job for my mother. It is interesting to imagine staying here with my baby. My mother hates to do laundry and my father always helps out in whatever way he can and he also washes his own socks. They hang up on the shower rod like skinny little cigars. They always look sort of lonely there, as if they wanted to be with the other laundry. It is better when my mother washes out her stockings and they hang up there next to Daddy's socks. My parents always wanted a big family, but my mother's insides could not stand it. Of course all this is pie in the sky, because I am married and my place is with Buddy.

The night we told my parents I was going to have a baby I said after, "We only did it once, we certainly won't do it again. Not until we're married." I was of course lying through my teeth. Buddy dug his thumb into my palm. We both kept a straight face which wasn't too hard. Those were the good old days.

$\mathcal{M}$y mother has a sick headache and my daddy and I are going to make breakfast for her for a surprise. This is just how it was when I was little on Saturday mornings. I always felt special but also a little embarrassed, I didn't want to act like an idiot in front of him. I tried always to have interesting things to say to him but couldn't always think of any.

"How does your mother appear to you, Virginia?" he asks, breaking an egg into the blue bowl. My father is very delicate and precise when he breaks an egg. I am sure he would have been a wonderful doctor. *Crack.* He breaks another one. Sometimes I think I could just sit here and watch my daddy break eggs forever, then whisk them with the little fork he likes to use. My daddy does not use the electric mixer. He prefers the old-fashioned way as do I.

"I thought she seemed a little tired," I say cautiously. This is always a safe answer.

"I was wondering if she wouldn't like a change of scene," says Daddy and for some reason this gives me a funny feeling. He is looking at me now. My father has the habit of looking at your cheeks, or the middle of your nose, but never your eyes. I have this habit too, which I inherited from him. If I remember to look in a person's eyes then I do but my gaze just naturally somehow falls to the middle of a face where you can't get into any trouble. And that way you don't really miss anything. You can get fooled by eyes but the whole face is easier to read. Anyway, it turns out that Daddy is thinking of taking Mother away for a while. Six months, maybe even a year.

"Where, Daddy?" I ask him. I feel cold all of a sudden. Like my bones are cold, it is the strangest feeling.

"Well, I was thinking of the Lake District. You know how your mother loves Wordsworth. I thought we might spend some time abroad." He puts a little salt and pepper in the bowl. Then he adds a tiny shred of water, which is my father's secret ingredient in scrambled eggs.

"Oh," I say, "that sounds wonderful." I put oomph into my voice.

"But of course," he says, "I couldn't do this unless I was certain that you were all right. Which is why I bring it up. Tell me how you are, Virginia. I would have to be assured that you were a reasonably happy young wife." And Daddy smiles at me his nice smile. The one that makes me want to jump into his arms and cry my eyes out.

"Oh, I'm fine, Daddy. I mean, we're all just fine. Really." I don't know what else to say.

Daddy puts the pan on the stove and lights the fire. "Well, that's good to hear." He put a big spoon of butter in and it begins skittering around. "That's very good to hear."

"When would you go?" I ask.

"We would be leaving possibly as early as September," he says, a note of excitement creeping into his voice, "and I believe we may have found a small house to rent. I would of course be expected to fulfill a few duties at the church in town, but aside from that I would have plenty of time to devote to what your mother likes to call 'roaming in the gloaming.'" Daddy looks so happy he might just start flying around.

"Oh, I think the change would be good for her," I say. "She has been looking a little down. I've noticed it myself." This is one thing I have in common with my daddy. We both keep an eye on the moods of my mother. It is important to both of us that she be happy.

"Well, she blames herself for your precipitous marriage, Virginia. She thinks it was somehow her fault. Your mother took it very hard, as you know." My daddy pauses here for effect. It's like one of his sermons where you feel guilty for everything, even what happened before you were born. "It has been hard for her to reconcile her hopes for you. It has been a difficult period of adjustment for her." I feel so terrible as he says this but fortunately here Daddy turns his back and pours the eggs into the pan. *Spatter* and then *gurgle gurgle*. He has a jelly jar ready for his last part, a big spoon of currant jelly in the middle. "I wouldn't want to leave if I thought you might need us here, although we will have a telephone and would expect to speak to you every ten days or so. We will also probably fly back once or twice during the year. Thanksgiving, perhaps. Easter." He drops the jelly on top of the eggs.

"Oh, Daddy," I say, "I think it is a wonderful idea. I think it is just wonderful. I'm fine, I'll be fine. I already am fine, thanks to you, of course," I say.

"Of course we will continue to send the money for rent, and if you find yourself in any financial bind I want you to let me know immediately. It is extremely fortunate that we are in a position to be able to do this." He is taking the eggs out now and putting them on the blue dish which is my mother's favorite. She will only eat eggs off this one particular dish. "I will tell her then that it is a go," says Daddy. "She has been worried about upsetting you. I am sure this will make her headaches ease up some too." I hold the kitchen door open for him and he takes the tray up to her bed. "Virginia?" my daddy calls in a low voice from the bottom of the stairs.

"What, Daddy?"

"You're a good girl, Virginia," says my daddy.

But I am not a good girl. I have never been a good girl. It makes me feel terrible that he thinks I am.

"Virginia?" My daddy came into my room that first night. Buddy had gone back home to New Jersey. I was just lying there staring at the ceiling, thinking this is not my room anymore. "This hurts like the very devil," is all Daddy said to me. He didn't rant and rave.

• • •

$\mathcal{D}$ot called. It was very nice of her. She said she thought we should be thinking about coming back soon. Everybody misses us, she said. Oh sure, is what I think. In that case why haven't I heard one word from Buddy? I did not however say that to Dot.

$\mathcal{I}$n celebration of their trip, Mother and Daddy and I go out for lunch at the Red Curtain. My mother is singing away, "A Foggy Day in London Town," and rubbing my daddy's neck the way she does. She has an excellent singing voice when she cares to use it. "Had me blue and had me doooowwn," she sings and I put the menu in front of my face and we all laugh because of how I used to be embarrassed by my mother when she was in a good mood. I get shot through with happiness when she is like this, although I keep a lookout for the first signs that it might be crumbling around the edges into a bad mood. Today however we have hit the jackpot. "This is where he wrote 'Tintern Abbey,'" says my mother, and shows me engravings from a book about WW, as my daddy calls him. "And I am certain we will find the exact cranny in the wall," she says, "where he wrote about the flower. Oh, Herbert, I am so happy, so happy," and I can see tears shining in both their eyes. "It has been so long since I set foot on that green and pleasant land." My mother is an Anglophile, to put it mildly. It is where all her ancestors came from four hundred years ago.

There are certain small cathedrals where she feels more at home than anywhere on earth. Daddy of course is not High Church, which has always slightly gotten my mother's goat. It is wonderful to see them so happy. They are still so much in love.

"I think you should get your passport updated too, Virginia," says my mother, unfolding her napkin and placing it in her lap. "It would be nice for you to come over for a while as well. Perhaps Dorothy could take care of Madeline, and we might all take a holiday trip to Paris at Christmastime." My mother refuses to call Dot Dot. It is hopeless to correct her so I never do. And besides, she is in a very good mood. I don't remember seeing her this happy in a long time. "Where is your passport, dear?" she asks. I have no idea, so I drop my napkin and pick it up and say I'll take a look and tell her when it expires.

My mother means this nicely, but of course I could not do that. I couldn't leave Madeline behind. Madeline is my baby! How could I possibly leave her at Christmas? For God sakes. But I can't say that as my mother would not understand. She is not so terribly sentimental about other people's families. I also could not just up and leave Buddy like that. Why does she think I could leave Buddy if she has never left my daddy?

After lunch my daddy goes outside to get an umbrella out of the car because it has begun to rain and I go to the ladies' room which is in the basement of this restaurant. I have been here a million times before. But this time as I am in the middle of washing my hands I suddenly wonder if I will know how to unlock the door. And then of course I dash over to the door and begin trying to get it open. The thing is I get mixed up and instead of unlocking the door I lock it again, and suddenly I think I'll never get out of here, nobody will ever be able to get me out of here and I look around and there are no windows, only a little vent high in the ceiling and I can't breathe and I begin pounding and pounding on the door and yelling, "Get me out of here! Help! Help!" just pounding and banging away and even when I hear someone outside I can't stop pounding. Finally I hear a deep voice say, "Turn the handle," and I do and the door opens and I fall into the arms of Martin Beeler who owns the Esso station and who had come down to "use the gents" as he puts it and "wound up with a pretty little miss in his arms." He must think I am out of my mind. Which of course I am. But he is very nice about it. "You're all right now," he says a few times, and he pats my back. Then I said I was fine and he went into the men's room. Nobody else heard, thank God, what with the noise from the kitchen, all those dishes and pots and pans banging around and I certainly don't tell my mother. She only knows about the kinds of problems you can fix with a damp cloth, or with a handkerchief and a little bit of spit.

Are you happy?" my daddy asked me.

"Oh, yes," I said. "Of course." How can I not be happy? Haven't I ruined enough lives? I have to be happy.

Tonight Maddie choked on a piece of popcorn and I nearly died of fright. I banged her on the back and it came up into her mouth. "Spit it out!" I kept yelling at her. "Spit it into Mommy's hand! Madeline!" and finally she did but she was very upset with me for yelling at her. I couldn't help it. She scared me half to death. It is terrible how many harmless things are dangerous for children. I just never really thought about popcorn. They should give you lists when you leave the hospital. Not everybody has common sense about every single thing. My mother put her paper down but she did not interfere.

"Oh, Mother," I said, "that was scary." I was trembling.

"Nonsense, Virginia," she said, picking up the paper again. "You coped."

Mother showed me the travel brochures and the photo of the cottage where she and Daddy will stay. It made me feel so homesick for some reason, I don't know why. I have never been to England. It made me homesick for my life. But Mother is so excited, and she loves to show me the little towns nearby, and the cathedrals she will see, and the places where William Wordsworth wrote and walked around. As far as cathedrals go, she loves the architecture and Daddy loves the services. So they will certainly make a good team.

I got Buddy on the telephone. It was midnight and I don't think he recognized my voice. "Who is this?" he said twice and then he hung up the phone. When I called back two seconds later there was no answer. Then there was a busy signal. Then Buddy answered it again.

"Buddy, it's me, Virginia," I said. "How are you?"

"Oh, I'm fine, Virginia," said Buddy, like we'd hardly met. "How are you? The baby okay?"

"Oh, I'm fine. The baby's fine too. She says 'Dada' a lot. We better come back soon or she'll be calling my daddy Daddy too!" I didn't mean to say this, it just came out of me. It isn't even true, which is what is so funny, because Maddie calls my daddy "Pop-Pop." Anyway, Buddy didn't say anything. So I said, "Just kidding. She knows who her daddy is and we look at your picture every night. 'Good night, Dada,' she says." I was making this whole thing up out of nothing. Buddy still didn't say anything. Then I heard like a snore. He had fallen asleep. I listened to that for a while, eavesdropping on my own bedroom. I kept thinking I heard rustles in the bed and once I thought I heard a sneeze but no sounds after. Nobody saying *gesundheit*. Thank God. After a while I hung up the phone. It was scary to stay on one second more. What if I suddenly heard Irene's voice telling

Buddy to scratch her back or something? What if Irene were right there in the bed with Buddy?

Dot called again. "When are you coming home?" is what she wanted to know. "We all miss you," she said again, which of course I did not believe. I could tell she thought I might never come back. I know Dot. It felt funny talking to her, sitting in my mother's living room with my mother sitting right by. I can't talk naturally to Dot if my mother is in the room. It's like I have to have very good posture. I felt all starchy and fake, I couldn't relax my voice and tell her what's been happening and how cute the baby is because my mother would stiffen up and get jealous. Which of course she would never admit. "I'll have to call you later," I say to Dot, "the baby is just waking up now. I'll call you later." Then I said to my mother, "Oh dear, Dot is very nice, but she certainly can talk," as if I were tired out by Dot which of course I am not. I love Dot. But I have to try and keep everybody happy and my mother just nodded and went back to her book. Danger averted! Later I called Dot when I was in the house by myself.

"Are they taking good care of you, Virginia?" is what Dot asked. I know she means well but I hate it that Dot calls my parents "they" instead of "your parents." And Dot doesn't understand exactly how families work. It always bothers me when she talks like this. My parents do things their way. It is really none of Dot's business how we act in my family. I would feel very angry if she accused them of doing something wrong which they certainly are not. I do not need taking care of as she puts it. I just need people to have good manners and behave in a civilized fashion, the way my family does. So I told Dot I didn't have much time to talk because my family were all going out some- where, which was not precisely true. My daddy and mother were going out for a drive and Maddie and I were home getting ready for beddy-bye. Then I heard Dot strike a match and that little sound she makes when she takes her first drag.

"Are you smoking, Dot?" I say. "I can't believe you're smoking."

"How did you know?" laughs Dot and then she coughs of course.

"Listen to that," I say. "Cough cough. Buddy's going to kill you."

"I'm only coughing because I've stopped smoking," says Dot in this serious voice. "You want me to stop coughing? Let me smoke a few butts. Buddy has no sense of humor about this." Of course this made me miss Buddy because the nicest part is how much he loves Dot. But I didn't want to talk about Buddy. I told Dot I missed her and asked how was Old Dog and said that we were both fine up here. She volunteered a piece of information.

"Buddy is going to try harder," says Dot. "He is going to apply himself more to his responsibilities. He's going to stay home more from now on. I have his word on that." Dot is talking in this hushed voice, as if she were giving me a box of jewels.

"Oh, Dot," I say, "that's so nice." I couldn't think of much else to say. Then she asked when was I coming home with her sugarplum. I said I wasn't sure, but maybe in a week or so. Did I have any message for Buddy?

"No," I say. "I spoke to him last night. Tell him he talks in his sleep."

"Last night?" asks Dot. "What did he say?"

"Nothing," I say. "I was just kidding."

"Old Dog is looking around for you," says Dot, yelling into the phone, the way she does at the end of a conversation, gearing up to say good-bye. "I swear he looks for you all over the house before he settles down on the porch."

We had a good laugh about Old Dog and then we hung up. I forgot to ask where Buddy was. Maybe he was right there, with his finger over his lips and shaking his head. I really did not care to know.

My daddy drove me and Maddie to the doctor this morning. Maddie was just lying limp and hot in my arms. I am not used to her acting this way, and her breath smelled sweetish and sick. The doctor was very nice. He listened to her heart and he looked down her throat, and he tapped her tummy and said she had the flu and there was a lot of it going around. "Nothing much to do except baby aspirin and plenty of fluids." He smiled at me. "Well, Virginia," he said, with his hands folded on his nice fat stomach, "look what you've gone and done. A pretty piece of work she is!" and I felt so proud of her and happy. He acted like it was the most natural thing in the world for me to have a baby.

Then later I was crossing the street and I heard someone yelling my name and there was Eddie running over and he said he had popped the question. He said I had inspired him to do it. And Yolanda said yes and he said it was entirely due to me and how happy I was in my marriage. "God," I said. "Well, that's great, Eddie," I said. But it made me stop and think.

Maybe I'm not so miserable as I think I am.

I told this to Daddy and Daddy said he was proud of me and what a good mother I am. He says I have made such a difficult thing look so easy and he thinks my marriage will stand the test of time because I am such a determined person. He said he was taking Mother away for a three-day holiday to the city of Boston, as she had been anxious to look at some good art and see a few movies. So I decided to go back to Hadley this weekend.

I called Elinor to say good-bye. I mentioned the fact that Buddy sounded strange on the phone the other night. I said how funny that your imagination could play tricks like that, I could swear there was somebody else in the room with him. Elinor didn't jump in and reassure me. But how could she? She doesn't even know Buddy, except from a photograph, and I never mentioned about Irene.

"His voice sounded funny?" she asked after a pause. "Funny how?"

"Oh," I said, "I don't know. Just funny. Distant."

"Deeper?" asked Elinor. "Sort of throaty?"

"Not exactly," I said, thinking this was a ridiculous conversation. "Maybe."

"I know what it is," said Elinor. "I know all the signs. He's turning back into a frog."

This made me laugh, imagining Buddy sitting on the pillow like that. A large green frog.

"Take care of yourself," she said and I said, "You too," and she said she would send me tons of letters and her address in case I ever felt like running away to sunny Italy. Then after we hung up I took a deep breath and I called Buddy. He said hello in a nice voice and when I told him we were coming home he said that was great and of course he would pick me up at the train and he didn't sound un-happy about it. He sounded almost nice, in fact.

I'm going back tomorrow. I am determined to make this work.

Kicking and screaming we lay waste our powers.

Part Three

The worst thing is that when the train pulls in I see Buddy but he is not scanning the windows for my face. He is just standing there looking at his feet, or the cement. I do not see Dot anywhere, and he has brought the Dodge which has the bad gasoline fumes smell and the first thing I say to him is, "I can't sit in the back." It just comes out of me. I wanted to say, "Oh, Buddy, it is so good to be home," and hope that he would fold me into his arms, but instead all I could say was I can't sit in the back. Buddy smiles at me a forced-looking smile and he kisses Maddie, who sticks her face in my neck out of shyness. "That's your own daddy," I say to Maddie, and pretty soon she peeps a look at him and he puts her on his shoulders and carries our bags to the car in one hand. Buddy is very strong and can easily carry two bags in one hand. He holds on to Maddie's feet with the other.

"Good trip?" he asks, when we are settled in the car. He looks so handsome but a little on the pale side and his hair is slicked back and you can see comb marks in it from the oil he has put on. I feel so flattered, like he has dressed up his hair to meet us. And he just recently shaved too.

"Great, yes," I say, "Madeline is such a good little traveler," and then I ask, "How are you? Where's Dot?"

"Dot?" says Buddy. "She's at home."

"I thought she'd come to meet us too," I say. He frowns at me. "I didn't mean it as a criticism," I say quickly.

"Well, Old Dog died," says Buddy. "She's burying him this morning. Under the porch."

"Old Dog? Old Dog died?" I can't help it, I start crying and pretty soon Buddy is crying too, little gasps but he won't look at me and when I touch his shoulder he nods but he keeps both hands on the wheel. For one second I hate Dot for having such an old dog in the first place who you just get attached to and then it dies. But then I realize this is mean and I am just so sad that I will never hear his clicky shuffle and feel him rest his chin on my foot again. I can't even believe it.

"But how can she get him under the porch?" I ask. "Old Dog was big." And I blow my nose on one of Maddie's diapers.

It turns out he died yesterday and they had him cremated and nobody called to tell me.

"Why didn't you tell me?" I ask Buddy now. "Why didn't you call me and tell me?"

"I don't know," says Buddy. "I just didn't think about it." He bows his head. "I'm sorry, Virginia. He wasn't your dog, I guess." That hurts my feelings worse than anything. We just sit there, Buddy with his hands on the wheel but without the engine on and me staring out the side window. Maddie on my lap just sitting quietly for once.

"How could you not call me."

"I'm sorry, Virginia," says Buddy. "Really." He says it as if he means he's sorry for everything. Everything, everything, everything. But it is a sorriness that takes him farther away instead of one inch closer and we drive home in the mood of a funeral instead of a celebration. It hasn't rained here in two and one-half months and a lot of the lawns are turning brown. I'd forgotten how hot it is here. The heat just blasts you like a furnace, even with the windows down in the car it is like a furnace. I take off Maddie's shirt and let her sit half naked in my lap. And I roll the window all the way down and close my eyes and let the hot wind blow in my face.

For some reason Dot got all dressed up to bury Old Dog. She is wearing her terrible black and white dress with the big floppy collar and the big strawberry-shaped buttons and the dreadful little cape that hangs down uselessly in the back. She is wearing red shoes. She has her hair in the little bun instead of flying loose in scraps and she has lipstick on as well, but her face is grimy from dirt and sweat and tears and her hands are dusty. "Poor Old Dog," I cry in her arms and she pats my back.

"Poor Old Dog," she says. "But he went easy. He went easy, Virginia, in his sleep."

"I wish you had called me, Dot," I say, "I wish I had known when it happened. I feel terrible that I was just going along not knowing for one whole day."

"I didn't want to spoil your vacation," says Dot, "I'm sorry. Here," she says. "Get some flowers. I'll hold the baby. You go get some flowers and we'll put them under the porch." So I do. Buddy and Dot take the baby and the bags into the house and I go back behind the garage where there is a patch of wildflowers growing. "I don't even know if you like daisies," I whisper, reaching under the porch to lay them on the little pile of earth. There isn't much of you left when you get cremated.

Everything is so clean. They have practically boiled the house, it looks so nice. I open the icebox and inside is tons of food and even food coloring and vanilla on the windowsill. A huge bottle of it. I know what this costs. "Oh," I say. "Oh dear, oh dear," and I know I can't start crying now, everything is just so confusing. I am not used to everybody being so nice and thoughtful suddenly. I don't know exactly how to act.

"I hope you rested up good," says Dot, coming in behind me, "because me and Buddy are expecting some nice home cooking from you. Isn't that so, Buddy?"

"Sure are," says Buddy. "We sure are." He is standing by the door with his arms crossed on his chest. Sort of hugging himself, his hands underneath his own armpits. He nods. "Can't wait for supper, in fact," he adds, smiling.

Well, this is very nice.

We drive into town for Maddie's apple juice. Everywhere everything is brown and dried up. Dot says we can't even water our gardens anymore. Nobody remembers a hotter summer. I just know you could fry an egg on the sidewalk, something I have always wanted to try. The first night back I make a big salad and some French fries. French fries are the only hot food you can stand in the middle of summer, I think. Madeline stuffs them in her mouth and Buddy likes his with mayo and plenty of pepper. It is nice to see him eat what I make, and we all have very good manners. I go to bed early, Buddy sits up late to watch the game but he is very nice about it. He isn't coming into bed with me and I don't care. I am just as glad. I had put my hand on his back but he just said in the nicest voice, "I'm pretty beat, Virginia," and I took it right off again. I can take a hint. I didn't even really want to. I just thought maybe I should.

Buddy has taken to playing his guitar again. I come upon him sitting on the bed just singing quietly to himself, not even standing in front of the mirror. Buddy loves ballads and knows many country-western songs and used to write them, too. Before we started going out he sang me a song he had written for his old girlfriend, who was of course Irene, and I had never laid eyes on her. It had a soft melody and the words were nice but sort of silly. "Oh Irene, your face so fair, with your love all things I dare to do, it's true" is all I can remember. I used to wish he would write a song for me, but he never has. I hope he is writing something for us. He comes home after work. He has been home every night this week. This is working much better than before. I am even hoping he will come up with a pet name for me. There isn't really a good nickname for Virginia, but I have thought Ginger might be nice. It sounds so peppy, sort of, and I wish he would think of it. I try different hints. Ginger ale. Gingerbread. I say, "Oh dear, are we out of ginger? Do you have any desire for gingerbread, Buddy?" But so far he doesn't take the hint.

$\mathcal{I}$ have decided to ask Irene and Chick for supper. It is my way of saying we are making a fresh start and I am willing to do my part. They are our friends, after all.

"Yeah?" says Buddy. "Are you sure? Are you sure you're up to it?" Well, that is kind of silly. Why wouldn't I be up to it, for God sakes. I just wish he didn't suddenly just perk up like that at the sound of her name. "Okay! I'll give them a call. Oh, when is good for you?" he asks.

"How about tomorrow?" I say. So now he is in such a good mood it kills me but I am determined to make the best effort. All day long I make my special spaghetti sauce and also a batch of brownies. I have pinned up a bunch of photographs of me when I was pregnant and one of the baby sitting in Buddy's lap. I put these on the cupboards, and on the walls. I put the big one of Buddy holding his newborn baby daughter right on the fridge where it is noticeable. This makes me feel safer, surrounded by all these factual photographs. "What are you doing?" asks Buddy, but he can hardly object. What can he say? All afternoon I am busy getting ready and Buddy hangs around asking if he can help and I tell him to set the table which he does, putting the forks on the right and the knives and spoons on the left.

Chick and Irene arrive at seven-thirty after Maddie has gone to bed. I am just taking the brownies out and Buddy has two fans going to try and cool off the kitchen and then we all four take a vote and decide to eat out on the porch anyway. Buddy and Chick set up the old card table and Irene lays the tablecloth on top. Then she comes into the kitchen and goes right to the fridge and looks at the photographs. "These two look very happy," she says, and I can't read anything into her voice.

"Yes," I say. "Well, that was certainly a happy time. Buddy was just in love with his baby girl." This was not strictly true. Buddy had a lot of trouble holding Maddie at first, and he wasn't good when she cried. He just had to leave the apartment. But it is a nice picture. He is holding her so carefully, as if she were a delicate vase full of beautiful flowers.

"Buddy-boy," says Irene, looking at all the other pictures I Scotch-taped up. "You're such a family man. How come I never knew?"

Buddy mumbles something I can't hear. He is carrying the silverware and plates out to the card table. Chick comes into the kitchen and grabs a few chairs.

"Smells like a million bucks in here, Virginia," says Chick.

"Why, thank you, Chick," I say and then turn back to Irene. She is looking at the one of me pregnant staring out my mother's living room window. "I was seven months along in that one," I tell her. "My daddy took the picture. Of course, Buddy was just so interested in the whole process. You know. The whole pregnancy." I have never actually used the word "pregnancy" before.

"Was he now?" says Irene, stepping away from the wall. Her arms are folded across her chest and she sort of leans back to regard me. I can hear the trace of an Irish accent for the first time from Irene. "Was he now." Like a flavor in her words. Irene has black eyeliner on tonight and she has a red scarf tied around her neck. It is sort of chiffon.

"Yes," I say. "Anyway, I've been meaning to put all those in the scrapbook Dot gave me but I just haven't had the time yet. So I thought I'd just put them up where we can all enjoy them." Chick comes back inside just then and as I throw the oven mitt toward the counter Chick intercepts it.

"High fly ball to center field," says Chick, "and he makes the catch!" Then he throws it to Irene, who throws it back to him hard. And that changes the funny mood in the air. Thank goodness for Chick. I have upset Irene somehow. All I want to say to her is this is my baby and this is my husband. That's all. But I keep rubbing it in. So then I ask her where she got her beautiful belt which has a silvery guitar for a buckle. It is unusual.

"Oh," she says, flustered, "I picked it up in Philly." She smooths her skirt.

"Well," I say, "it certainly is a beautiful thing. I would love to go to that store sometime myself."

Then Buddy comes into the kitchen. "How long before we eat?" he asks me.

"Oh, ten minutes?" I say.

"You two okay?" asks Buddy. He looks from one to the other of us. We both nod. Then he scrambles around in a drawer for the church key. He opens a can of beer and quickly sucks up the foam. "Sure you don't need a hand with anything?"

"No, Buddy," I say. "We're doing just fine." Then Irene sneezes and goes into the bathroom to blow her nose. A sneeze is the punctuation of a true remark. If you say something and somebody sneezes right after, that means it is underlined for truth. So I guess we are all right so far. I drain the spaghetti over the sink and hold the colander up for a while to let all the water out. Chick comes over.

"Wow," he says. "Lots of that, huh." Then he takes the lid off the big pot on the stove where my sauce is. "Goddamn," says Chick, rubbing his hands together.

"Chick, if you'll just bring me the big yellow bowl, please, over there on the table," and I jerk my head back and he gets it and holds it while I dump the spaghetti in. "Thanks," I say. "Do you think we should put the sauce right on or serve it separately?" Chick just shrugs helplessly.

"Whatever you usually do," he says. So I stick it in the big red bowl and put a ladle in.

"There," I say, "now all we have to do is bring it outside and we eat."

"Soup's on," Irene announces in a loud voice, holding the screen door open for me and Chick, who is carrying the yellow bowl. I have the sauce.

"Man walks into a bar, head the size of a golf ball," Buddy says, when we are sitting at the table and I am giving everybody their spaghetti. Chick puts his hands over his ears.

"People are eating," Chick protests.

"After dinner, Buddy," says Irene. "Save it."

Well, I hate it that she is telling my husband what to do

so I say, "What? Man walks into a bar with a head the size of a golf ball what?" but Buddy is already joking around with the Italian bread, pretending to duel with Chick, and Irene is sprinkling parmesan on her food.

"This looks good," she says. "Real good." She looks at Buddy. "I think your wife was speaking," she says. "Listen up, Buddy." And she smiles at me then takes a bite of salad. Irene is a nice person, I have always known this.

So then I try to tell my Santa Claus and the mouse story but it turns out they don't even know I am telling a joke which is very embarrassing. So I ask them to tell me some old stories about what they did when they were young, what kind of scrapes did they get into and so forth. I wanted to know more about my husband I say, and I pat his knee which feels unbelievably brazen. Nobody says anything at first. They are all thinking.

"Tell her about the time we broke into the Embassy Club," says old Irene finally.

"God," says Buddy, "that was a hoot and a half." He seems so relaxed now. I miss Old Dog all of a sudden, out of nowhere I start to miss Old Dog.

"Speak for yourself, Buddy," says Chick with half a smile.

"What happened?" I say, but I already hate that Irene was part of this story. I hate to think of the three of them running all over having adventures like the damn Three Musketeers. They have known each other so long. It makes me jealous. The only people I have known longer than two years are my parents. I wish Old Dog had his muzzle on my bare foot right now.

"We broke into the Embassy Club," says Irene. "It's downtown, you know it? The big cinderblock building? It's like a Moose Hall, if you know what they are, they have parties there for firemen and cops. Well, Chick stole the key from his dad's jacket and we broke in around eleven in the morning and found that tap. Beer was on tap and I knew how to tap a keg and we were drinking our asses off when we heard somebody opening the door downstairs. Man, was I scared," says Irene, brushing her hair out of her eyes. "Me and Buddy got out the back window and ran up the hill."

"You were still carrying your glass of beer!" says Buddy. "You wouldn't put your glass down!"

"Damn straight, it was a perfectly good glass of beer," says Irene. "I don't waste beer on tap," she explains to me, as if I were a ninny, "and we scrambled out a window in back and ran up the hill and got away. Chick got caught. He tried hiding out behind the bar. Actually," says Irene, looking fondly at Chick, "you were too bombed to move."

"Then what happened?" I ask. I take a swallow of my ice water.

"Chick got caught. His father beat the shit out of him."

I must have looked shocked because Chick spoke up.

"Well," says Chick, shrugging, "that was his job."

"But you were just a child!" I say, truly horrified.

"Chick was already full-grown at fourteen," says Buddy. "All five foot ten of him."

"I don't think that's funny," I say to Buddy.

"It didn't make an honest man of me either," says Chick. "I didn't give up a life of crime until I discovered girls. Not sure I made the right decision," he says, and gives Irene a little poke. "Not real sure about it sometimes."

Nobody says anything and I notice it is exactly eight-twenty.

"This always happens at either twenty of or twenty past the hour," I announce after checking my watch.

"What always happens?" asks Irene.

"Don't get her started," says Buddy, groaning in a friendly way.

"If a room falls silent," I explain to Irene, "it is always either twenty of or twenty after something. No one knows why."

"Is that true?" says Irene. She opens a can of Dr Pepper, her favorite drink. I have bought an entire six-pack of Dr Pepper for Irene.

"An old wives' tale," says Buddy, still shaking his head. "One of many, Irene, you wouldn't believe it."

"You'll see," I say confidently. "And Buddy, you should talk. You walked around knocking on wood the whole time I was pregnant." I beam at him. "Don't you remember? You didn't walk under your ladder either, not that whole last summer." Everybody is quiet again. You could hear a pin drop.

"Well, Buddy," says Irene. "You're a thoughtful guy." She gets up from the table suddenly. "Ice," she calls without turning around. "Soda's getting warm out here." Buddy gets up too.

"What is it, Buddy?" I call. "Do you need my help?" I am really acting like a wife tonight.

"Cheese patrol," says Buddy. "It's under control," he calls through the screen door. "Out in a second." When he comes back, Buddy is carrying another bowl of parmesan cheese.

"Man comes into a bar," he says, as soon as he sits back down.

"Here we go," says Irene, who has just come back too. Her glass is filled with ice cubes. Her face is pinker than usual and she looks happy. I like watching everyone eat what I have made. It gives me a great feeling of happiness mixed with power.

"Head the size of a golf ball," Buddy goes on. "Bartender says, 'Excuse me, sir, but you must get asked this all the time. I can't help noticing that your head is an unusual size. Is there a story behind it?' " By now Chick is groaning and Irene has her fingers in her ears. Really Buddy is just telling this joke to me since I am the only one who hasn't heard it before but I don't think he realizes that fact. It would embarrass him to tell me a joke all by myself.

Well, it turns out the man had been walking down the beach and he found an old bottle and out of it popped a genie who was a very beautiful woman and she tells him he can have three wishes. First he asks if he could sleep with her and she says no, she is sorry, but that isn't a wish she can grant. Then he asks if he can maybe just make out and she says no, she is sorry, that isn't a wish she can grant. So finally he says, "Well then, how about a little head?"

I laugh so hard I think I'll die. I double over laughing. It just strikes me the funniest thing I ever heard in my life.

"It's not that funny," says Buddy.

"Yes it is. I love it. Maybe you are all just used to it." I have to wipe my eyes and blow my nose. "A little head," I say and start laughing again.

Buddy acts all miffed. "It isn't that funny," he repeats but all I can do is laugh. "Get ahold of yourself, Virginia," he says. "God."

"Well, why did you tell it then if you didn't expect people to laugh?" I am wiping my eyes on my apron.

"I just didn't expect my own wife to laugh so hard."

"I notice women prefer this joke ten to one," says Chick. "It's a female thing. Irene thought it was pretty funny, didn't you, Irene," he says.

"I did," says Irene. "The first two hundred times. I've just heard it to death is all. You're being a prude, Buddy. Virginia can laugh at anything she wants." By now we are all finished. I am planning to make espresso by using a lot of instant coffee in the tiny cups. But first I think we should relax further and I decide to tell Elinor's joke.

"I know another really good one," I say. "There's this old Italian man named Luigi," I begin, but Buddy interrupts.

"Hey, Virginia, whoa," says Buddy. "Ease up. Chick's grandma is Italian. We don't do Italian jokes here."

Chick winks at me. "She was Italian," he says. "No point in denying it."

"Well, in this one the Italian comes out on top," I say. "It isn't a mean joke." But I don't tell it. I wouldn't want to hurt Chick's feelings.

It is nice sitting outside and Irene and I talk about cooking a little, although she doesn't cook much except sloppy joes which apparently Chick loves. And Chick is working down at the garage. He is an excellent mechanic. He owns a 1953 Cadillac with some special kind of engine. He has been fixing it up and he and Buddy go on and on about that. We eat our brownies on the porch. They don't stay late. Chick says it was the best food he has ever eaten in his entire life, which I think is very nice of him. Irene nods. "Fabulous," she says. "I ate two brownies." Chick ate five. Then Irene sneezes three times in a row and Buddy jumps up and gets Irene's shawl from the kitchen and he puts it around her shoulders. Her shawl has red roses all over. This puts me in a bad mood. Whose husband is he, anyway?

They drive away and I go into the kitchen to start tidying up.

Buddy comes trotting up to the porch. He was out on the driveway looking for shooting stars. I have told him you can make a wish on a shooting star and it is the only thing he seems to believe in. Thank God it's bad luck to tell your wish. Suppose I tried to worm it out of him and it turned out he wished he had never met me and was now married to Irene and Maddie was their baby.

"I thought Irene looked a little tired tonight," I say to Buddy. "I guess that's why they went home so early."

"She's a hard worker. Those dogs give her a lot of grief. She puts in a full day," says Buddy. Irene never complains. Buddy complains for her.

"Oh, really," I say, placing the red bowl on top of everything in the drainer. He hates it when I do that. Buddy likes things symmetrical. By this time I am mopping up the card table and rinsing out a napkin that has wine stains on it and I am feeling extremely nasty. I hate it when Buddy acts as if I don't do anything or know anything. As if I am not a strong person with a real life. I have a baby, don't I? How easy is it to stay home, does he understand that? He wouldn't last one day in charge of Madeline. He'd have to go to a rest home. Buddy is in a good mood, I can tell. He is humming away under his breath. I guess he thinks we had a wonderful time. We did, until he put the damn shawl on Irene. That ruined everything as far as I'm concerned.

"Since when did you get so concerned about Italians, Buddy? You're the one who's always saying 'wop' and I'm the one who's always correcting you." I knew I was picking a fight but couldn't help myself.

"That's different," says Buddy.

"Exactly how is that different?"

"I don't want any wife of mine telling a dirty joke, Virginia. I don't even like how hard you laughed. You're a mother." He stops drying a glass in order to look at me for emphasis. Sometimes direct gazes cause my eyes to water and they do that now. There is nothing I can do except turn my face away. "What's with you? Are you going to ruin a nice evening?" He sounds impatient. I can't stand it when he sounds impatient, as if he were my father.

"Oh," I say. "I get it. So it's okay for you to say 'wop' and 'guinea' and tell a dirty joke and it's wrong for me to tell a colorful humorous story with an Italian in it and wrong for me to laugh at a funny story all because I'm Maddie's mother?"

"You got it."

"Well, piss on that," I say which shocks me, and I go into

the bathroom and slam the door. Pretty soon I hear the screen door slam and Buddy's car start and him drive away. So I come out of the bathroom and start slamming the front door over and over. I just slam it ten times in a row. Slam it and open it and slam it again.

"What's going on?" calls Dot, the light coming on over the garage.

"Oh, nothing," I call to her. "Nothing at all. Tra-la-la."

Then the outside stair light goes on and pretty soon there is Dot in her nightgown and curlers and cold cream all over her face carrying her big flashlight.

"Did he go out again?" asks Dot. She looks all worried and keeps wiping the hair out of her face but it's sticking in her face cream. Poor Dot. "Is the baby okay?"

I look at her. "Yes he went out. We had a tiny fight. And of course the baby is okay. Why wouldn't the baby be okay?"

Dot pats me on the back. "How about my special sure-fire cure for everything?" says Dot, shuffling over to the cupboard and rooting around for the eyecups and the bottle of Benedictine.

"Oh, Dot," I say, "thank you. But I'm just going to go to bed. I'm sorry I woke you up. It was all my fault anyway. I got in a bad mood for no reason." So Dot goes home, but I have to pretend to push her out the door to get her to leave.

Madeline is still asleep. She inherited this from her father.

The next day I find out that Buddy spent the night parked in the school parking lot sleeping in his car. That was pathetic and sad. Dot got to him first, before I was awake. By the time I got up with Maddie he was sitting at the kitchen table and there were two cups of coffee in the sink and Dot's cigarette smoke was everywhere. He said he was sorry and I said I was sorry and we made a truce. "It was a great meal, Virginia," Buddy said to me finally. That cheered me up. I didn't mention the shawl.

$\mathcal{I}$ got a letter from my mother with their itinerary. They will be leaving in two weeks, and flying to London. From there they will hire a car and drive to the Lake District. She has included a map of England drawn by her, and she is an excellent artist. At each city there is a picture of the famous person or church associated with it. She has done a beautiful job. She has even drawn herself and Daddy waving at me from England's shore. "We will miss you, Virginia," the figures are saying in a balloon over their heads. In the envelope is also a check for five hundred dollars. This takes care of five months' rent.

I call her up to say thank you but Daddy answers the phone.

"Your mother is shopping," he says. "She says I need luggage. I told her my suitcase is fine but she says I need what she calls proper luggage," and he laughs his little loving laugh about her.

"Well, I called to say thank you for the moola," I said, because sometimes my daddy and I joke about money this way. He is not so straitlaced as you might think. He can relax. Once I saw him with one of those pens that you turn upside down and the woman's bathing suit comes off. I watched him standing there turning the pen upside down and right side up a few times, looking at it with such a comical interested expression on his face.

"You are quite welcome," says Daddy. "You're fine, aren't you, dearie-pie?"

"Oh, I certainly am," I said. "We are all fine. And Buddy is looking forward to going back to school, too. Buddy is just so serious about making a go of everything. He is doing very well on his summer school course, too. He thinks he will get an A."

"Well, that's all very good news," said Daddy. "I'll tell your mother you called. *Je t'aime*," said Daddy. He likes to say "I love you" in other languages. I don't think he has ever said it in English. Of course Buddy never says it at all.

"Je t'aime aussi," I said and we hung up. In our family we generally use French for love and Spanish for death. *"Muerto"* is what I say if I come across a dead animal in the road. I never think the word "dead." *"Muerto"* is a beautiful

word, with possibilities in it still. "Dead" just lies there. You wouldn't want to poke it.

$\mathcal{B}$uddy and I went to the movies one night, Dot babysitting for Madeline, and we saw *Rebel Without a Cause*. I sat as close to Buddy as I could without making it obvious and I leaned my head toward his the way you do when you're out with somebody you like. He didn't shy away but he didn't make a move toward me. He didn't put his arm around me either. But he was very polite. He didn't recoil. "Can you see from here?" he asked because he likes to sit way in the back. "Oh, yes, Buddy, this is perfect," I said. So we watched the movie and I tried to eat my popcorn very quietly as I am certain that crunching sounds annoy him. When it was over I said, "Oh, I just think that is the dumbest thing I ever saw. Although the acting was quite good." I turned to him. He was looking for his jacket which had fallen between the seats. "Don't you?"

"I didn't think much about it," said Buddy.

Then we went out afterward for a sundae and it was terrible because I couldn't think up any conversation except Maddie. "Maddie is growing up so fast," I said. "Just every day she is doing more and more. Can you believe she'll be one whole year old in just three weeks?" Buddy shook his head. "A whole year of being a father and a mother," I said.

"Really, did you ever imagine such a thing in your wildest dreams?"

"Not really," said Buddy, playing with his ice cream but not really eating it.

"Well, I'm just so glad it all happened this way," I went on, "because it gives us so much more experience, don't you think? I mean we're not so superficial as other people our age."

"Who are you talking about?" he asked, sounding irritable, and so I clammed up. Besides, suddenly I wasn't sure who I was talking about. Or who he was talking about either. I got very absorbed in something to do with my sundae. And the thing is once you know you are irritating a person everything you say comes out irritating. So finally I said, "Are you going to eat that or can I?" because if they're going to hate you they're going to hate you and you might as well eat their ice cream. He pushed it across the table at me. "Thanks," I said. I didn't even care that every sound I made was probably driving him crazy.

"Hey, I'm sorry, Virginia," said Buddy. "I've got a lot on my mind."

"Well, what?" I asked. "Tell me." Licking the back of my spoon.

"Oh, it's school. Nothing specific, thanks for asking," he said. I tried to hold hands with him across the table but instead he reached for his wallet. The waitress had just brought us the check.

"What? Do you want to stay in Hadley?" I asked. Maybe he was homesick at the thought of leaving. I could understand that. But he just shook his head.

"It's not important," he said.

"It's important if you're miserable," I said.

"Who said I'm miserable?" He sounded angry. "You read too much into things, Virginia, you exaggerate. That's why I can't talk to you."

"Oh, is that so," I said. "Okay," I said. "Okay, you're happy as a lark. Fine. Great." And I got up from the table and waltzed out the door, grabbing about twenty after-dinner mints as I did. These are Dot's favorite food and she loves it when I bring them home for her. Buddy and I didn't say one word driving home. I threw the mints out the window one by one.

"Well, did you two lovebirds have a good time?" asked Dot when we got home. It was so embarrassing. "Did you watch the movie?" This is Dot's horrible joke.

"Crummy movie," said Buddy. "Cornball flick, that's all." And we took the baby and went home.

It is too bad marriage doesn't come with attachments like a vacuum cleaner. You can't do anything with ours. Ours just sits there and blows hot air. It isn't good for anything at all.

The first time a boy touched me I was wearing a dress with a lace collar and no shoes. We were parked at the beach and by accident his hand flicked across my chest and I thought I would die from it, just die right there in the car. He began to apologize for accidentally touching me but I didn't say anything, and his hand went back there and hovered, I could tell, but I didn't say anything, I just turned my face to get another kiss, and he put his hand down on my breast. I thought I might possibly die from that pleasure, I really thought I might possibly die. We didn't dare move and spoil everything so we just stayed frozen like that, his hand on my breast and our mouths together, as if we were holding our breath underwater. I let him keep his hand there I don't know how long and then we moved and he began apologizing left and right and I said it was not his fault, and then afterward, when I was home in my room, even though I knew better, I was afraid I might somehow now be pregnant. As if just the shocking pleasure could do it to you. It makes me so sad sometimes to think I will never have these feelings again since I am now married.

Buddy is restless. After supper he tries to read the paper but five minutes later he starts prowling around. He can't sit still. Outside it is a warm purplish night and Buddy needs to be driving around in it. But he is trying, I can tell that much. "Do you want some lemonade?" asks Buddy, getting up and going into the kitchen. "Why thank you, Buddy, that sounds very nice," I say. It is like having a wild animal try to cook. He's just a lion who is trying to behave. All he wants to do is run around outside.

"I'll make some," says Buddy and I can hear him sawing away at the lemons and "Where's the sugar?" he wants to know, and then I hear the ice cube trays coming out again and going as usual all over the place.

"Buddy," I say when he brings me a glass, "did you put any water in this?" and he looks horrified and we pretend to have a good laugh but then that's done and he flops back down on the old brown couch that is stained with every imaginable thing and pretty soon he wants to watch the game but I am reading so he says he'll run down to Townie's and watch just an inning or two and come right back. So I say fine, because by now it seems like the best thing. But he doesn't go. He just sits around rattling the newspaper looking at car ads. So then after a while I go to bed and Buddy turns on the television set. "Helps me unwind," he says. "I'll be in in five." In this way we don't have to lie next to each other and do nothing until one of us is asleep. I haven't even seen him in his underwear since I got back. He goes to sleep in his clothes and wakes up in his clothes and only takes them off in the bathroom. Well, that's okay with me too. I am a very modest person anyway. I never get naked in front of Buddy. I just get in the closet and pull the door almost shut when I'm putting my nightgown on. He used to joke about that in the beginning but not anymore.

This morning Buddy was standing with his back to me and I saw something dark, like a stain on the skin of his left shoulder. "Buddy!" I cried. "Are you all right? Did you hurt yourself?" He looked nervous and wheeled around and pulled his undershirt on fast and yanked it down. It fits so tight across his chest and his arms just bulge out of the sleeves. He always looks so good in his undershirt, actually, that was what he was wearing the day I met him. I came barreling across the room like an idiot. "Let me see, Buddy," I said, "I think I have a right to know if you've hurt yourself." It was scabby, but when I got close enough I realized it was a tattoo. A tattoo! I could not believe my eyes. "Buddy," I said, "you went and got a tattoo after all, for God sakes!" Buddy nodded and tucked his undershirt into his jeans. "What is it of?" I asked. "Really! Show me!" I thought maybe he had put a heart with our initials in it after all and was embarrassed to say it. He mumbled something.

"What?" I said. "Really, what? You can show me."

"It's a rose."

"It's a rose! That's nice," I said and then my face fell. I remembered that Irene's name is Irene Rose Mahoney. "You call this a rose?" I said.

Buddy nodded, putting his workshirt on and starting to button it wrong.

"Isn't that somebody's middle name?"

"It was the cheapest that's all."

"How much was it?"

At first he wouldn't tell me. "Nothing much," he said, but he looked guilty.

"You tell me I can't buy damn vanilla and you go out and get a tattoo? How much was it!"

"Fifty."

"Fifty *dollars?* That includes the ink?" I laughed. "Is this why you sleep in your damn clothes? You think I'd never see this? Did you think I'd never notice?"

"I didn't think about what you'd think," Buddy said. "If I decide to get a tattoo that's my own business." He started to comb his hair like everything was hunky-dory. Just these long, suave I-don't-care-what-she-says movements of comb-ing, one hand holding the comb, the other patting his stupid hair into place. "I can't tell you every move I make. You were in Wellfleet, anyway." Comb comb.

"Who did this?" I said, in an icy-cold voice, "because it is a very amateurish job."

"Oh, friend of a friend," he said. "Guy in Philly." And he just kept combing his hair.

I acted like I couldn't care less. I acted like it was just the most boring thing I ever saw. Then I said very casually, "I

wish you had done this professionally, Buddy." I almost said
Buddy-boy. "Because it looks like a big old boil. It doesn't
look like a rose. It looks like there's something wrong with
you. It looks like cancer."

Then I walked out of the bedroom and started rattling
the pots and pans. I didn't know what else to do except
make a lot of noise.

𝒥 thought he was going to try so hard," I say to Dot, and
stamp my foot. "Do you know what he went and did? He
got a tattoo!" Dot looks surprised. "He did. He went and
had Irene's name tattooed on his shoulder."

"Get out!" says Dot, sinking into a chair. She put one
hand over her eyes and the other over her heart. "I don't
believe it."

"Hope to die," I say. "He has a rose tattooed on his
shoulder. Forever! You know they never come out! That is
Irene's middle name! How do you think that makes me
feel?"

"It's a rose?" Dot looks relieved. "The flower? Oh honey,"
says Dot, "I think you're making a mountain out of a mole-
hill. That's just Buddy showing his independence. You know
how men are." And she goes back to vacuuming. "I thought
you said it was the name." She starts shoving the couch
around to get underneath.

"No, I do not know how men are, as you put it, Dot,

and I hope I never do. I don't see how you can just happily vacuum away when it is obvious that Buddy is in love with Irene."

"Calm down, calm down," says Dot, patting my arm. "Calm down, Missy."

Well, my name isn't Missy and I won't calm down.

Dot gets our clothes out of the hamper and throws everything in the washer. "You don't have to do that," I say, following her around.

"Buddy likes his jeans folded down the middle," she tells me, like it's something I need to know.

"Let him fold them himself," I say.

"Virginia," says Dot, using her soothing furry voice that reminds me of pouring syrup all over everything, "there is always a period of adjustment." What does she know? She has never been married. "You have to give him a little time. Everything will be all right, Virginia, just have patience. Buddy is a good boy. Wait, you'll see."

I get good and sick and tired of that talk. I have never spent so much time waiting around in my whole life. I don't even know what I'm waiting for.

Yes I do.

I'm waiting for something to change.

I turned the radio on this morning. It's my old radio from home, the one I had when I was little. It is made of white plastic and has the shape of the Lone Ranger molded right in, and the little speaker has gold threads among the brown and all it plays is AM but that's all I listen to anyway now. Rock 'n' roll. This morning I was dancing in the kitchen with Madeline. Her face gets as pink as mine does, and she laughs that funny laugh with her chin digging into her chest and when we do a really fast move she looks almost frightened but it is just excitement. She likes it best when we pretend to do the tango, holding our arms out straight and following them around the kitchen like a boom mike. I consider dancing to be a very good form of exercise and I am usually worn out after half an hour of good tunes. Today they played "Blue Suede Shoes" and "Honey Don't" back to back and these are two of my favorite songs to dance to and I had taken off everything except my bra and shorts because of the heat and Maddie was sliding around in my arms and then it was Jerry Lee Lewis, "Whole Lotta Shakin' Goin' On," and I can go low in that song, quite low. I learned to do the limbo at college. That is the sum total of what I learned, how to do the limbo and how to tie a cherry stem into a knot inside my mouth. You have to have pretty long stems. It was considered very sexy.

I was dancing away like a crazy person and I looked over at the door and there was Buddy standing outside for how long I do not know. I was so nervous. He hates me dancing. I kept hold of Maddie who covered up the front of me as my bras tend to be on the dingy side. "Buddy, gosh," I said, "I didn't expect you home at this hour."

He came into the kitchen and first thing he did was turn off the radio without asking.

"Is this what you do all day, Virginia?" he asked in a cold voice. I wondered what he was doing home at eleven-thirty in the damn morning but I was too nervous to ask. I was up against the sink, actually, attempting to put a superior look on my face but I was hampered by being very sweaty and out of breath and also holding the squirming Madeline who of course wanted to get down and dance by herself. "Yes!" I felt like shouting. "It's all I do all day long!" Instead I snapped the radio back on. I know it was childish of me but I couldn't seem to help it. "Tutti Frutti," but I didn't move at all.

Buddy looked upset but he didn't say a word. He stared at me until my eyes began to water. Then he turned on his heel and walked into the hall and I saw him pick up the phone. Of course with the radio on I couldn't hear who he was talking to but I couldn't exactly turn it off now. I had to prove my point. On his way out of the kitchen three seconds later he said without looking at me, "Car broke down on the Etra Road. Mulford's coming by to pick me up. Please turn that thing down until I'm out of here." So of course I did. It was a reasonable request. His voice sounded so tired and he had paint in his hair. I always imagined marriage where you would gently take the paint out of the other person's hair but I could never touch Buddy now.

I watched him through the curtains while he waited in the driveway. He stood with his arms around himself looking at his feet, his head bent down. The paintbrush was sticking out of his back pocket now. After about five minutes a truck pulled up and Buddy climbed in and they drove off without glancing even once at the house. I watched the whole time through the window. I felt so unfinished, I don't know how to describe it. The next thing I knew there was Dot patting me on the back. "He got so mad at me," I said.

"Oh, Virginia," said Dot. "There, there. He's just wrought up. And I'll help you do those pesky dishes." But it isn't her job, it's my job. Only I never seem to get around to it. I like to cook, that's all I like to do—cook—and sometimes I like to scrub the sink but that's all.

"Do you want me to talk to him?" asked Dot, with her back to me. Her mustache is always darkest at the end of the month. She bleaches it on the first. You can tell the day of the month by Dot's mustache.

I shook my head.

"I'll set him straight," said Dot, her lips disappearing into her face. "He washed out his own coffee cup when he was a bachelor. Why should he expect somebody else to do it for him now?"

It seemed funny to think of Buddy as a bachelor. He isn't old enough to be a bachelor. Dot and I cleaned the kitchen and then we sat around and chewed the fat as she puts it. She is on vacation one day at a time. "Too much might go to my head," she says, "but one day at a time I can handle. What say you, me, and Missy here go down to the Mr. Chicken for a little lunch?" Well, that was so nice of her. I hate Mr. Chicken, it is so greasy, but Maddie loves it and it is nice to get out of the house.

I don't think it should be Mr. Chicken anyway. Mr. Chicken would have to be a rooster. But that is what is so sad about Hadley. They also have a fat woman's clothing store called Le Belle Femme. I don't want to tell them how wrong that is. Besides, it kind of reminds me of Dot's mustache. It usually makes me smile.

That night when Buddy comes home we pretend nothing happened and the whole kitchen is clean. And I make a lemon meringue pie which I know is his favorite and he eats half of it. I feel much better.

I hardly ever catch sight of Buddy's tattoo. He always wears a T-shirt. I think this is because I said it looked like a birthmark or a skin disease and I think that sticks in his mind. Words are as indelible as tattoos in their own way. Anyway, it doesn't get on my nerves as much as I thought it would. You can get used to anything, I guess. You can choose what will tick you off and what won't, Dot says. I am choosing not to be concerned about it.

I had a bad dream that I was standing outside the library at home with a big bag of potatoes and then the bag broke and I had to pick up all the potatoes which kept rolling away. I know it sounds funny but it was a terrible dream. They kept rolling into the street which was full of cars whizzing by. Buddy said, "That's what you call a nightmare?" and that was all he said. No wonder I never tell him anything.

The car is in our driveway now gathering dust. It still won't start. But it isn't just the battery. Buddy gets picked up every morning by a couple of guys in a truck who drive him to work. They don't always get him home exactly on time either but of course it isn't his fault. They go down to Townie's and watch a couple of innings after work. Chick came over this morning to take a look under the hood. He is so good with cars. He doesn't even have to do this, it is his day off. Poor Chick, he came in the middle of my bad mood.

"Can I come in?" he asked, after he had fooled around with the car awhile.

"Now why would you want to do that," I said, holding the door open for him.

"You're a nice person, Virginia," said Chick. "Why

wouldn't I?" Well, that shows how much he knows. I am not a nice person. I am about as far from being nice as you can get. "I was kind of hoping you were in the middle of making brownies," he said.

"No eggs," I said. "No walnuts." I open a few cupboards and then slam them shut. "See? Nothing." *Slam*. "See? Nothing here either," I say, *slam slam*. I am in a very bad mood.

"Having a hard day?" asks Chick, but it is a nice personal question.

"Well, sometimes I just want to stamp through the floor I get so frustrated with certain people."

"Buddy is a horse's ass," says Chick, but not unkindly. This is the second time he said such a thing.

"Well, I don't see how you can say that and still be his friend," I say.

"I'm a horse's ass too," he says, and laughs. "Anything I can do to cheer you up?"

"Oh, Chick, I don't know," I say. "I always pictured everything so different. I always though you'd be able to laugh and cry in each other's arms when you were married. Don't you want to be able to cry your eyes out in somebody's arms?"

"Well," says Chick, "I'd much rather not. But if I have to, I have to."

This makes me laugh, of course. "Do you really want brownies, Chick? Because we need eggs and walnuts."

"I could get them for you," says Chick.

"Well, maybe something sweet would be a good idea," I say. "Let me see if I have everything else," I say, and start rummaging through my baking shelf. I certainly still have plenty of vanilla. "Do you know what I feel like?" I ask Chick with my back to him.

"What?" says Chick.

"I feel like a piece of slimy old parsley in the veggie drawer."

"Oh," says Chick, "I don't know. I've always been partial to parsley myself."

I turn around and he smiles at me. I guess I've never seen Chick smile before and it is really very nice. It is kind of a crooked smile, one side of his face goes up and the other stays put, and lines come in like a lot of parentheses beside his mouth.

"Oh," I say, blushing in spite of myself. "Well, you have a very nice smile, Chick, you should smile more frequently. Really. I think it may be your best feature."

"Shucks," says Chick, which is one of my favorite words.

"No, really, I mean it," I say. Chick starts fiddling with the sugar spoon. "Oh, don't do that," I say quickly. He looks as if he is about to ding on a glass with it.

"What? What am I doing?"

"Don't do that with a spoon. It kills a sailor," I say. "I don't know why, it's just bad luck for them so I try never to do it."

"Where do you get that stuff?" asks Chick, putting the spoon back in the sugar bowl.

"What stuff?"

"That sailor stuff. That twenty of or twenty after. Where do you get it from?" asks Chick. "I never heard any of it before in my life."

"Oh," I say, "mostly from my mother, I guess. But a lot of it is just like in the atmosphere."

"For instance," says Chick. "Tell me what to look for."

"Well," I say, "for instance I knew you were coming today before you got here. Of course I didn't know if it was you, exactly, but I knew a man was coming because I dropped a knife." Chick looks at me expectantly. "That's it," I explain patiently. "If you drop a knife it means a man is coming."

"What means a woman is coming?" asks Chick. "If I go home now and drop ten spoons does that mean I'll have ten lovely ladies at the door?"

"You aren't taking it seriously," I say. I am looking at all the old spices in their little cans.

"No, I am, I am," says Chick, and he leans back in his chair and puts his hands behind his head. He is wearing a green T-shirt and I have just never noticed about his arms before. And then, like an idiot, while I am looking at Chick I stick my finger in the cinnamon tin and it gets stuck there.

"Damn!" I say, and I start hopping around the kitchen. "Ow!" I am cradling my right hand in my left.

Chick jumps up. "What is it, Virginia? Did you cut yourself?"

"Oh, Chick," is all I can say and then I close my eyes because I can't stand to see it if a look of alarm comes over his face.

"Yes, Virginia," says Chick, "you've got a problem here." I can feel his hand holding my hand.

"Don't say that."

"We can fix this," says Chick, moving me sideways over to the chair.

"What are you going to do?" I open my eyes.

"You just hold still," says Chick, and he reaches into his back pocket and brings out the tiniest pair of scissors I ever saw in my life.

"Where did you get those?" I ask him. "Do you just carry them around with you all the time?"

"Hold still."

My stomach is starting to growl which is terribly embarrassing. "I didn't eat my breakfast this morning," I say, "because the toaster is broken." Then I just sit there trembling with my eyes closed again. I can feel him cutting away on the tin.

"That pinch?" asks Chick, pausing for a second. "I don't want to hurt you."

I shake my head. My stomach starts to growl again, of course, so I have to talk some more.

"You know once I got my knuckle stuck in a napkin ring. It was terrible, I couldn't get it out and I thought I'd have to spend the rest of my life in there. The shop teacher sawed me out. His name was Mr. Rickles. I screamed so loud they heard me in assembly. That was in Hannibal, Missouri. We lived there once for two years. For a few months after we moved my friend Karen Rasten and I played Monopoly through the mail. Then we sort of lost touch."

"Is that so," says Chick, snipping away.

"Yes," I say. "It is so. It was our favorite game." My eyes are still closed.

Chick doesn't say anything, he just keeps snipping.

"Okay," says Chick at last, "you're out."

I look at my finger which is none the worse for wear, just a small crease along the top joint. "Thank you, Chick," I say. "Oh, thank you so much," and I stand up to hug him. He is holding the remains of the cinnamon tin in his left hand so only his right arm is free to hug me back. His body is nice and warm like a big alive chimney which surprises me and I let go right away. Then Chick goes to throw the snippets of tin in the trash and brushes the cinnamon off his hands into the sink. His back is to me.

"Chick Chick Chick Chick Chick," I keep saying. "You saved my life."

"Steady hand and a pair of snips. All it takes." He turns and watches me with his head on one side with a funny little smile.

"I'll make brownies, Chick, and you can eat every one. They are all going to be for you. Go on. Shoo!" I say to him. "Go get some walnuts!"

"I'll have to take a rain check, Virginia," he says, and he looks at his watch. I am so disappointed.

"But then how will I ever repay you?" I ask.

"Ah," says Chick. "Never ask a man that question." He pauses as if he is waiting for me to say something jokey but I don't know what to say. So then he says, "Show me how to make spaghetti sauce. If I bring the tomatoes, you show me how to make the sauce. Deal?"

"Deal!" I say.

Then he lifts his imaginary cap and goes out the door. Chick has an imaginary cap the way some kids have imaginary playmates, I think.

"See you later, Virginia," he says. "Take it easy." Chick can make even "take it easy" sound so friendly and personal. He is a very nice person to have around from time to time.

"See you later too," I call after him but he doesn't turn around. Then I rush into the bathroom and dot my cheeks with lipstick and rub it. I need a little color in my face. "You are an idiot," I say to myself in the mirror. When I come out Chick's car is gone.

I am very sorry to see him go.

I saw Chick and Irene this morning. She waved but she didn't stop. They were going somewhere in the truck. Chick waved too, but he didn't turn his head to watch me as they passed. I got jealous that Chick was in the truck with Irene. Everybody has someone to be in a truck with, and none of them is me. The other morning Buddy got his car towed down to the garage. Chick fixed it and didn't charge anything for his labor. Buddy was ticked off because he thought Chick could have done it right here in the driveway. "Don't look a gift horse in the mouth," is what Dot said. I think Chick thinks I am too silly to be around. He was probably afraid I'd come out with cinnamon tins stuck on all ten fingers or that I would make him eat an entire pan of brownies. Well, who cares, is what I say. I bought some more cinnamon.

The toilet won't stop flushing and Buddy keeps saying he'll get to it but meanwhile just remember to flush the handle up not down. Well, I can't always remember that so now I have put a big sign on the seat and I keep the seat down so that I won't forget. But once in a while I automatically flush it the wrong way and it flushes away for about ten minutes which can drive you crazy. Plus we are in the middle of a drought. I don't see why we can't just call the plumber but plumbers cost money says Buddy and he knows how to fix it, it's just a simple part. Well, if it's so simple why doesn't he do it? Because he's asleep half the time, that's why, and the other half he's out again.

Maddie and I are mostly left to our own resources which is fine with us. We fill up the washtub out back, which is illegal I am sure because of no rain for so long, and we make little boats out of sticks, and we look for caterpillars and put them in a mayonnaise jar. We found those bristly brown ones which I never minded touching when I was little but now I have to scoop them up with leaves. I don't know why as you get older you can't touch certain things anymore. Maddie will touch one's back and then shiver with a funny look on her face. We take walks downtown and sometimes we sit under the big copper beech where nobody can see us because the branches and leaves hang down like a big red cave. But mostly it is so hot that we just hang around the house. There isn't anywhere to get cool. We sit in front of the fan and pretend we are flying through space.

I got a postcard from Elinor. It is a statue of two men wrestling and one of them is upside down and has a tight hold of the other one's penis. I couldn't believe my eyes when I saw what they were doing. I don't know how this made it through the U.S. Postal Service, honestly. But it is very funny. "Dear Virginny, How's by you? Life is just a bowl of cherries over here as you can tell by this card! Ever thine, E." Then she writes a tiny P.S. "As for Luigi, I'm thinking of breaking it off. The wedding I mean." I put it away before Buddy got home as I do not think he would understand Elinor's sense of humor. I wonder how she is really.

It hasn't rained here in seventy-three days. The local paper keeps track. Even the corn is withering in the fields and all the news is full of don't water this and don't water that. One shower per day, et cetera. It is so brown here and all I can think of is home, and the blue ocean and the green trees. A couple of firemen came by today. At first I thought they had found out we filled the washtub up for Maddie but they were selling raffle tickets for the fair. At the end of the summer they always have a big fair with a Ferris wheel and other rides and they are raffling off a car. I never win anything but I bought two tickets for fifty cents apiece as the men were very nice and one of them had curly red hair and green eyes. I was thinking how did that happen way down here in the middle of nowhere, red hair and green eyes, and then the other one said Maddie was the spitting image of her daddy and he gave me my change. All I had was a five-dollar bill I'd been saving. I did not realize they knew Buddy. Then after they left I imagined the redheaded fireman coming back and sweeping me into his arms and telling me he had fallen in love on the spot and wanted to take me to Tahiti where we would raise Madeline and eat breadfruit.

$\mathcal{D}$ot is home for three days this week. She has bought a bunch of clothes for Madeline and two skirts for me and a yellow blouse which has a horrible bow. I have to put it on to make her feel good but I wish I could just tear it up for rags. She is excited to be taking me and Maddie to the lake for a swim. I hate lakes. I don't swim in still water. This particular lake doesn't even have a name as far as I know and it is the kind of water that when you come out you are a little brown and slimy. There isn't very much of it because of the drought but there is enough for people to get wet and go crazy. Somebody has a big red ball they keep throwing out in the middle of this sorry little lake. Hooting and hollering as if they were in paradise.

"This is very nice, Dot," I say to her because I have good manners and because this is Dot's vacation and I am not about to spoil it for her by being in a bad mood. We have brought a basket of food. There are a lot of people here, and a raft floating out in the middle and a diving board off the raft. There are tons of people swimming, if you can call it that, and sunning themselves, and lots of little kids

running around with ice cream smears on their faces and
ice cream drips on their little naked chests and mothers
hollering after them. I am suddenly so homesick for the
nice white sand and big blue ocean of home. I am filled to
the top of my head with homesickness.

Dot and Maddie go for a walk over to the swings. I can
see their two backs, Maddie's little brown back and Dot's
skinny white one in a terrible suit with crisscross straps
that shows poor Dot is as flat as a board. Dot is having a
nice time. She loves being a grandmother. I am sitting on
the blanket pretending to read. There is so much noise. At
home it is just the ocean but here it is people shouting at
each other. At one point I even think I hear Buddy's voice
but whoever it is dives into the lake and stays in the water
on the other side of the raft. I get up and go down to the
water anyway just to check because I think I keep hearing
somebody shout Buddy's name. But of course all the action
has died down as soon as I stick one toe in the water.
Anyway, there are probably plenty of people with dark hair
who go swimming in their white T-shirts. And the next
thing I know, as soon as I am back sitting down on the
blanket there is Irene of all people. She is dripping wet and
doesn't even have a towel so I hand her one of ours. My
heart beats fast and I try to gauge from the way she looks at
me what she is thinking—You poor thing, you are so far
from home and everyone is in love with me. "Hey, Vir-

ginia," is what she says, "Chick hasn't stopped talking about your brownies yet."

"Hi, Irene, your suit looks so good." I sound so calm and friendly I amaze myself.

"Who'd you come with?" she asks, looking around. "Been here long?" She dries her hair with the towel. Irene looks better without makeup but I can't mention this fact to her.

"Dot brought us on the spur of the moment. Buddy is working this afternoon. He will be sorry to have missed it though. He loves to watch his little girl." I can't help myself, I shade my eyes and point to the swings where Maddie and Dot are squawking happily away. "They are just inseparable, really. Except of course, like now, when they aren't together. He is really a devoted father, all right." Then I feel terrible. Why do I always talk like this in front of her? "It's such a nice day, isn't it?" I say, grabbing on to weather. "God. Not a cloud in the sky."

Irene turns to look at the water and a bunch of little kids go running past and they kind of froth around her chasing each other then they race off toward the lake. "Hey," I say, because maybe she is lonely, and I pat the blanket next to me. "Want to sit down for a minute? Want a sandwich? We're loaded with food here." I open the picnic basket. "See?"

"Thanks, not for me. I had a hot dog awhile back." But

she does sit down, sort of gingerly, as if the blanket might be booby-trapped. So we sit there and it is really quiet between us so I say, "I thought I actually saw Buddy diving off the raft two minutes ago. I know that means something but I can't remember what. When you see somebody's double, you know." But Irene is still looking at Madeline and Dot playing on the swings. "How's the water?" I ask her.

"Oh, you know. It's your basic swamp. It's wet, that's about all I can say for it." Irene keeps staring at Madeline.

"Hey, you know what?" I say suddenly. "You are one of the nicest people in the whole state of New Jersey. I just thought you should know that." And I sort of put my arm around her shoulders.

"Hey, yourself," she says, smiling a little. "What's with you? Sun going to your head?"

"No, really," I say. "You have always been so nice to me. Really."

Irene frowns. She puts her arm around me too and we sit like that. It feels awkward but in a nice way. Then Dot turns around to yell something I can't hear and her face changes when she sees Irene. She pulls Maddie off the little swing and heads back to the blanket, Madeline kicking and screaming and wriggling in Dot's skinny strong arms.

"Where are you going?" I say to Irene, who is on her feet.

"Got to run, Virginia." She waves at Dot and Maddie without stopping and plows right into the water. I can see her swimming out to the raft they've got floating in the middle. She's got a strong kick.

Dot fusses with the picnic basket and doles out sandwiches. "What was Irene doing here?" she asks.

"I guess she's got a day off too," I say.

Dot starts combing Maddie's hair with her own black pocket comb. Maddie sits very still for this as she is the only child I have ever heard of who likes to have her hair fixed. "She thought she had Buddy sewed up tight," says Dot, "and then he met you, and I thank my lucky stars he did. You are a wonderful influence on him, Virginia. Not to mention a certain small person we both know," and she pats Maddie's head. How can Dot say such a thing? I am not a wonderful influence on anybody. It makes me nervous when Dot talks like this. Fortunately five minutes later Dot gets hot and we pack up and go home.

I vacuumed under the bed and something caught and it was a can of Dr Pepper with a candle stuck on top all burned down to nothing.

"Is this yours?" I asked Buddy. He was in the bedroom too, looking for a pair of socks.

"What are you talking about?" he said. "What?" I shoved the can under his nose.

"I'm talking about how did this get under our bed."

"Don't ask me," says Buddy. "How the hell should I know?"

"I'm serious, Buddy. I demand an explanation."

Buddy doesn't hesitate one second. "God, Virginia. What's your problem? Chick and Irene were over while you were gone. We went to the lake and came back here. We had a blackout and used this for light. Blackout lasted maybe half an hour," he said looking at the candle.

"And what is it doing under our bed?"

"I have no idea," said Buddy. He is staring hard at my chin when he says this. "I really have no idea." He brightened. "Maybe Old Dog took it under there."

I narrowed my eyes. "Oh, I'm so sure," I said. "You have an explanation for everything, don't you, Buddy." I am still holding the can. "Dr Pepper, Buddy, who drinks Dr Pepper around here?"

"You're looking for something to worry about, Virginia. You have too much imagination," which is what he always says.

I just can't imagine myself out of here, that's my problem. If only I could imagine me gone. There are people who have worse lives. People live with people who hurt them, who beat them up and throw them out of windows. All I have is a husband who happens to be in love with his old girlfriend. I don't blame him. I like her much better than I like me most of the time. So there we were standing in the bedroom and I didn't know what to say what with so many thoughts flying around crashing into each other like little berserk airplanes in a tiny sky. What if Irene really was here in our bed when I was away? What if they are sneaking around seeing each other all the time? Suppose that was Buddy yesterday and Irene just came over to distract me? Buddy took me by the shoulders then and backed me over to the bed.

"Sit," he said and he sat down too. "Listen. I know what you're talking about. We're friends, me and Irene. We've been friends a long time. I can't just cut that off, can I? You wouldn't want me to turn my back on a friendship, would you?" He took a deep breath. "I'm married to you, Virginia. We're going to spend the rest of our lives together. Doesn't that satisfy you?" Buddy smelled like a big peppermint.

"Actually," I said, "that's the worst thing I ever heard. You don't even love me." And I got up from the bed and went outside and sat on the edge of the porch with my legs dangling in the tiger lilies.

"Hey," said Buddy two seconds later, sitting down next to me. "Hey. I'm doing the best I can." He put his hands between his knees as if he were praying and he leaned forward so his body was bent over. I could smell sweet oil on his hair. "Maybe I'll get better at it. Hey. I've got to get better at it. Can't get any worse, can I?" He was trying to make a joke. "Smile, Virginia," he said. "Come on, a little smile."

But I just couldn't.

Now I look through his pockets when he falls asleep. I am waiting to find a scrap of paper with Irene's name on it, or who knows what that will prove that he loves her. He has stuff in his closet, too, from when he was in high school and I am planning to look through that too one of these days when nobody is around. It makes me sick to my stomach, but I know he loves Irene. So far all I have found is gum wrappers.

What shall we get Madeline for her birthday?" Buddy asks me. "What do you think she'd like?" He is being as nice as he can. He sounds innocent and eager. This means he must feel guilty.

"Well, I don't know, Buddy," I say. "I'll try and think." But a whole week goes by and we haven't discussed it again.

He buys her a teddy bear and I buy her a pink blanket and a tiny little white pillow shaped like wings.

Dot took the baby and I was going downtown by myself this morning and walked past the park and there in the distance I saw Buddy and Irene together and they didn't see me. I couldn't speak. It was like a spell was cast over me and all I could do was watch. They were sitting at a picnic table and she had her elbows on the table and her head in her hands just leaning forward broody and he was leaning sideways toward her talking, with his face in the frown he gets when he is saying something serious nicely (which with me is never) and he was talking and once in a while she nodded. I was too far to hear what he was saying thank God. Usually it is Irene who talks constantly and Buddy just tells jokes around her. Then she said something and wiped her eyes and he almost put his arm around her shoulders but stopped short. I could tell because it's what I don't do with him. Probably she froze up and he knew it. He just sort of hung there a minute, not knowing what to do, then he patted her back. I would have patted her back too, anybody would have, I can't hold it against him. Then I noticed a puppy playing at their feet chewing on Buddy's boot and they both looked down and laughed, and then Irene looked up and saw me in the distance and she waved and I waved very energetically, as if I were in a big rush, and I even pointed toward town and then at my watch and hurried away like the rabbit in *Alice in Wonderland*.

I thought about it all afternoon. They just leaned toward each other as if the other were their sun. They made it look so easy. I never know what to talk about. I only know what not to talk about.

Buddy came home early and he was in a quiet mood. I

didn't ask anything about what he was doing with Irene. I didn't want to know, to be truthful. I bet he was telling her about Madeline's birthday or something and it just threw her for a loop. But I could never ask. He looked as if he were afraid to touch anything. He could hardly stand to hold the iced tea I made him, I could see how he just needed to put it down so softly on the table and how he touched the spoon as if he had never seen a spoon before or a sugar bowl, putting its lid down carefully. He smoothed Maddie's hair out of her eyes and when I suggested we cut her bangs he said, "Okay, sure," and we did. He pinned a towel around her shoulders and she loved it, and he sat her on his lap in front of the big mirror so she could watch, which kept her sitting very still while I cut her bangs carefully. I was just so close to him. I know he could breathe my breath as I could breathe his.

"You need two people to do this," I said. "It's just impossible with only one. Thank you so much for helping. Do you think I'm cutting them too short?" and I stopped and stood back to look. I had done one half and they seemed a bit short like a monk's tonsure without the bald spot.

"No," Buddy said, "it looks great," but he looked sad, and put his face down on top of her head so I couldn't see his expression. I felt sad too, I don't know why. Probably because we were being so nice to each other. The one person who had a good time was Maddie. She sat ever so still with such a serious important look on her face and watched in the mirror. When I finished cutting we shook the towel with her curls outside so the birds could make nests with it, which was my idea, and then Buddy held her up in the air and she squealed, she loved it, and then he even gave her her bath, and put her into bed. I could hear him singing "I've Been Working on the Railroad." When he came out he gave my shoulder a squeeze for no reason. This mood lasted for about an hour and then he went somewhere in the car. When he came back he got into bed with me with only his shorts on. I felt him touch my shoulder and breathe in my hair. I turned around then sort of overly fast because I was happy but also somewhat alarmed since we haven't done anything like this in a hundred years but when it came right down to it, Buddy couldn't. It just wouldn't work right for him. I felt so terrible. I know he felt terrible too. He kept saying, "Don't worry about it. Don't worry about it, Virginia, stop apologizing. It's not your fault. It has nothing to do with you." That of course didn't sound good to me either. You want it to have something to do with you even if it isn't working. So it ended up worse than before. I didn't know what to do. I didn't know what to say.

The day I got married my mother cried and cried. She just could not stop crying. She put her face on my daddy's shoulder and he just patted her back. I smiled as best as I could but then I started crying too. There was nobody there but me and Buddy and my parents and Dot and Chick, who was Buddy's best man. I didn't have a maid of honor, we had just done this as a quick wedding down in New Jersey where my daddy does not even wear his minister's collar. I had to get the borrowed and blue things myself. My mother just could not manage. Now I know what she was crying about. Marriage is just awful.

It is Madeline's birthday and everybody is on their best behavior. Buddy is cleaned up and wearing almost a suit and I have on the horrible blouse Dot bought me only I have cut off the bow. Chick is also dressed up very neatly in a pair of chinos and a blue shirt with a necktie, of all things. "Chick!" I say. But then I don't know what else to say. I am feeling so bad for so many reasons I really can't smile. We are at the Embassy Club where Dot gets a discount and there are streamers and party hats all over and Maddie is having a wonderful time blowing her little horn.

"Hey," says Chick, touching me under the chin, "it's a birthday!"

"Oh," I say, "I know that."

This is Dot's party and she has chosen the menu. We have hamburgers for our main course, and they are all cooked down to nothing, the way Dot approves. Plus mashed potatoes and broccoli with melted Velveeta poured on top. It is disgusting but I have to say Maddie loves everything. The cake will come later.

"To the best little baby in the world," says Dot, and I look at Irene but she is raising her glass too, smiling and talking to Chick, who is leaning over to hear every word she says. Buddy clinks his glass with mine. "Happy birthday," he says and I clink him back. "To Madeline," I say. I wonder if Buddy remembers the night Maddie was born. When it was all over and they let him come into my room and he had just seen his tiny new baby, he said, "Oh, you wonderful girl," and he bent over the bed and kissed me on the lips. It was very nice, I have to say, but it disappeared into thin air that feeling. It was like a one-time thing.

Madeline is a perfect birthday girl. She is busy stuffing her little mouth with mashed potatoes. It is sort of like spackling. Sometimes I think I could just watch Maddie eat forever. She has gotten so good at it. In the beginning she would get a whole bunch of food in her fist and then stick her fist in her mouth but then she couldn't open it and would just have to take it out again and then cautiously open her hand to see what was in there and try the whole thing again. Most of it went down her arm into her little sleeve when she had a sleeve on. She had a little kimono my mother bought her and so much food used to collect in the sleeve. Today she is wearing her pink dress with the frills and I swear to God she looks like a birthday cake herself, just as I predicted. But everybody is behaving so nicely. I am talking to Dot, who wants to talk about baby clothes, and after a while I have to use the ladies' room.

"Where is the ladies' room?" I ask Dot and she points down the hall.

"Down the stairs," she points, "past the kitchen and take a left by the telephone." It sounds as if it is in the bowels of the earth, as Elinor would say. How appropriate. "You can't miss it," says Dot, and we transfer Maddie to her lap.

I go down the stairs and there is Chick coming up them and it is very bad luck to pass somebody on the stairs so I stop. Chick stops too. Maybe he thinks I want to talk to him. "It's just bad luck," I say, "to pass on the stairs. That is why I'm stopping." And I brush my hair out of my eyes sort of haughtily.

"Uh-oh," says Chick. "What do we do now?"

"One of us has to move," I say. "We can't both do it at the same time. You go first."

"What if every time you move I move?" Chick asks, fooling around. Chick fools around too much.

"Oh, Chick, I'm not in the mood for kidding around," I say. "Now wait until I'm at the bottom, okay?" and I brush past him to go downstairs. "You are never serious about anything," I call back up the stairs. He is still right there in the middle. "You probably aren't even coming for your cooking lesson."

"Yes," says Chick, "I haven't forgotten that." Oh sure, I want to say. Tell me another.

And then of course I'm faced with this horrible bathroom with no windows and I just wedge my shoe in the door so it won't close and pray nobody comes down and nobody does. Then I put the shoe back on my foot like Cinderella and go upstairs. The cake comes out shaped like a big pink bunny and Maddie's face is astonished, and we all blow out the two candles and she keeps blowing three or four puffs after they are out, all two of them, and then we all clap. "Hooray for Madeline!" we all shout and she is so happy and I wish everything else were all right.

The weather broke yesterday but you'd hardly know it from today. It rained and rained but they say the earth is dry two feet down so everything just got all drunk up in no time. But maybe it will start getting more bearable. I get a postcard of a little church in England from my mother. "Dear Virginia, Your father and I happened upon this place yesterday afternoon. It is so beautiful, so simple that its only ornament is it own shadow. Do try and think about Christmas. It would be good for you, we are sure. Hoping this finds you well, love from Mother and Daddy."

That's how my mother can talk sometimes.

I dreamed there was a prince right downtown in Hadley and I saw him in the movie theater in a big crowd and our eyes met and then he disappeared. So then I started hanging around the movies hoping to see him again because when our eyes met we knew we would fall in love. This was not a good dream to have when you are already married but I can't help it. So I was asking people did they think it was meant to be? Will I see him again? Was it meant to be? Did they think it was meant to be? It was a silly dream. So in my dream I called up Elinor and she said, "Look at it this way. If it happens, it's meant to be. If it doesn't, it isn't." Which is really a very interesting way to look at it.

*O*ut of the clear blue sky Chick comes over with a big bowl of tomatoes from his garden. I am so surprised and happy to see him. "Long time no see," I say for a joke, because Maddie's birthday was just a few days ago.

"How do these babies look?" asks Chick proudly.

"Beautiful, Chick," I say, taking the tomatoes out of the bowl and setting them on the counter. "They're still warm."

"Just picked," says Chick. "Five minutes ago they were hanging on the vine in the sun."

"Well, that's very nice," I say. I line them up in a row. There are ten of them, ten nice big fat tomatoes. I love how they look. "How did you grow these? Ours got all black from the drought."

Chick put his fingers to his lips. "Midnight watering," he says. "Creeping around by the light of the moon."

"You *are* still a criminal," I say smiling at him. "Wow."

It turns out Chick has always wanted to know how to cook. Spaghetti sauce is a great place to start because it is a cinch to make. Nothing is easier than spaghetti sauce made from real tomatoes. All you need is garlic and olive oil and tomatoes and wine and the secret ingredient which I never tell anyone.

"Of course, Chick," I say. "Now is perfect. I would be delighted. I am so glad that somebody appreciates my efforts in the kitchen." I am not actually prissy. I just sound that way sometimes. I don't know what happens to me.

"First you scald them, Chick," I say, setting a pot of water on to boil.

"Ouch," says Chick. He comes up behind me and looks over my shoulder. I can feel him breathing on my hair so I step over to one side.

"Nothing to it," I tell him. "You just stick a pot of water on the stove. You don't even have to salt it or anything. Just plain old water." He is still standing right next to me so I say, "Shoo, Chick, sit down. I'll tell you what we do next. A watched pot never boils, don't you know that? Beep beep, Chick, sit down." And I give him a very small poke with my finger and he sits down like he's been shot with a gun, clutching his heart he staggers back to the chair and falls down. "Chick," I say, trying not to laugh, "you are being ridiculous." And I put the tea water on too. "Want a cup of tea while we cook?" I ask.

"Iced tea," says Chick, "if it isn't any trouble."

Well, iced tea is trouble, actually, and what with one thing and another I forget to make it, the tomato water starts boiling, and I have to drop the tomatoes in sliding them off a spoon so as not to get splashed. "Now I have to wear an apron," I say, "but I'm sorry I don't have one big enough for you." I am embarrassed about this apron now. KISS THE COOK.

"These are old clothes," says Chick. "It don't make me no nevermind." I know he is fooling when he talks like this but I love the sound of those words together.

"Then it don't make me no nevermind either," I say. And I nearly skip over to the icebox and I begin to feel ridiculous. I feel like one of those ladies again opening her icebox door with a huge smile on her face. Well, this is certainly not real life, so cut it out, Virginia, I say to myself. This is Chick. This is not your actual life. So that sobers me right up.

"You have to scald them so you can slip them out of their skins easily," I inform him. But I feel sort of funny. It always feels a little sexy doing that to a tomato. I don't know why, it just does. I hope he won't think this is like sexy cooking and I am trying to get him or anything. But after all, it was all his idea. It isn't my fault.

"First you drop them in for a minute and then you take them out and run them under cold water so you won't burn yourself, and then you"—I put one in my hand—"squeeze it really gently and see? The skin slides right off and there's the nice tomato!" I look at Chick but he is watching seriously. I guess he does not have a really dirty mind which I am sorry to say I don't know where mine came from. I don't even know what it reminds me of. It just feels sexy to me, that's all.

"Then you take a knife and you chop them." I show Chick how to chop up a tomato by first making slices that don't go quite through, then making crisscross slices that just turn the tomatoes into small messy squares. "Don't throw any of it away. The seeds are good too," I explain, putting them all into a bowl. "Now, do you think you want to learn how to chop garlic? It's pretty difficult at first, but it's something you need if you're going to cook. Chop." I get the big knife out and I give him the head of garlic. "Separate all those little cloves. Just break them off gently. Good." Chick does this really well. "Now you have to peel them and that's hard because it gets sort of sticky. You just take a really small sharp knife," and I demonstrate by peeling a few. Chick watches carefully. Then I hand him the little knife and eight cloves of garlic. I hate peeling garlic, it takes so long, but Chick does it carefully and he does a neat job. "That's really good, Chick," I say, "you're a natural." It is nice to watch his hands because they are rather bulky but they can do such delicate little motions with the knife. When he is all done he puts the knife down.

"Now what?" he says.

"Now," I say, "the chopping. The trick is always to leave the point of the knife on the table. You just raise the other end and bring it down, see? Up and down and up and down, but you leave the point on the board, you never lift it off. Chopchopchop."

Chick tries and can't do it.

"Here," I say, and I put my hand over his. This feels funny, I am sorry to say, because Chick's hand is unexpectedly warm and it feels so amazingly muscular, I don't know how to say it, it just feels so strong closed on the knife like that. I make the motion of chopping. Up and down, up down. "Leave the point on the board, Chick," I say. "Just tiny little motions, you don't have to kill the garlic." Of course the garlic sticks to the sides of the knife so we have to keep stopping and wiping the garlic back onto the board and I decide this is too advanced and say so. "I didn't realize how hard this is, Chick," I say. "I think this is too advanced."

"No, no," says Chick. "Really, I think I'm getting the hang of it."

"All right," I say, and we keep chopping but I am feeling funnier and funnier because of how I can feel so much strength in Chick's hand without him really even making a muscle and I take my hand off his. "Well," I say finally, "that's enough of that. It doesn't have to be chopped up completely fine," I say. "It's not actual mincing." Chick is just sort of staring at me. He has a smile on his face.

"Let's do that again," he says.

"What? Let's do what again?" I say, pretending I don't know what he is talking about.

"You know. Chop. Don't you have anything else around here that needs some chopping?"

"Oh, Chick," I say, feeling warm and really very peculiar, "Oh, Chick, maybe this isn't such a good idea. I don't really feel so well and Maddie is going to be waking up in a minute and what I'll do is finish this and bring it over later. There's nothing to it from now on. Really. Just throw it in a bunch of olive oil and brown it up and then throw the tomatoes on top with some wine and cook it for a few hours."

But he looks so disappointed that I say, "Okay, okay. You heat up the olive oil in a big black frying pan." And then I hear Maddie start the snuffling grunts that means she's waking up. "Here," I say, "when it's hot throw the garlic in, but be careful not to burn yourself. And then turn the heat down." I go into the bedroom but Maddie is still asleep. I stand there a couple of seconds and hear Chick go into the bathroom.

"Flush it up," I say in the hall, knocking very gently on the door. "If you flush it down it just keeps flushing for hours. Okay?" And I go back into the kitchen and stir the garlic around. Then I hear this cackling laugh from the bathroom and the sound of the toilet flushing. "You've got to see this, Virginia," I hear Chick call and then laugh hysterically again. It flushes again and I start yelling.

"It's not funny, Chick, it will just do this for hours!" and I go barging in and he is just standing over the toilet looking into the bowl. Flushflushflush.

"It's like a magician taking rabbits out of a hat!" says Chick. I look in. It is exactly like a magician taking rabbits out of a hat. Rabbit after rabbit after rabbit. Little strange fat water rabbits. It is kind of fascinating, and funny, and I start laughing too and there we are both of us staring into the toilet and I say, "It's more like a magician putting rabbits *into* the hat, Chick," and then I look at Chick and he looks at me and we both stop laughing.

"Why did you get married, Chick?" I say. "If you don't mind my asking."

"Well," says Chick, "truthfully? I wasn't doing anything else at the time."

"What?"

"Irene wanted to get married. We've been friends a long time. I wasn't real busy."

I can't believe my ears. "You did it to be nice?" What a terrible reason to get married.

"I'm not nice," says Chick. "I'm easy."

"But you do love her, don't you?" The toilet miraculously stops flushing.

"A man should love his wife, don't you think?" says Chick, beginning to smile, and I feel I am getting out of my depth. With Chick you aren't always sure what you're talking about so you have to be careful. Then I look at him again and it is like a shock. He puts his hands on my shoulders. "See you later, Virginia," he says. And then he goes home fast.

Oh my God, is all I can think of. Oh my fucking God, as Elinor would say. I almost kissed Chickie Freund.

This is excellent spaghetti," says Buddy, who is on his best behavior for no reason I can figure out. "Excellent. What is your secret?"

"Oh," I say, "I always put in a little cinnamon at the end. It gives it a little history. I don't know. It just gives it a little history."

"Delicious," says Buddy, helping himself to more. I never noticed before but Buddy sort of snaps his food off the fork. Like a trout. He just brings it up in front of his mouth and then he snaps at it. "Chick and Irene asked us over for a barbecue," says Buddy between bites. "How about it? Want to go?"

"Sure," I said, which surprised him I think. "Why not?"

"By the way," says Buddy. "I had an interesting talk with Mulford today. You know he sells houses on the side."

"Yes?" I stir my tea with a fork.

"He said he knows of a house that's going to go cheap, real cheap, and soon. He says he'll advance me the money in return for me fixing it up. I'll work off the down payment and buy it from him cheap. Works out good for everybody."

"What are you talking about? Where? Here?" I put my fork down. I am suddenly terrified.

"Over by the old post office."

"Not that run-down thing on the corner?" I can't believe we're having this conversation. I feel like I'm in a dream.

"It could be fixed up real nice," says Buddy. He is so excited he is even leaning across the table toward me.

"But Buddy, you're still in school. Why would you want to do this now? I think it's a terrible idea." I realize I haven't ever thought exactly about where we might actually live. I can't possibly live in Hadley. It's just out of the question. I'd rather be dead.

"I can work on it vacations. Winter, spring, summer. I

can have it fixed up in no time. I graduate, and presto, we've got a place to live." He wipes his plate with a piece of bread. Now I know why he's in such a good mood. "It has a great porch," he says, as if that were all I wanted in life.

"Excuse me, it has a rotten porch. It is completely rotten. And it has no windows and it has no roof on one side. You expect me and Maddie to live there?" I still can't believe this is even a possibility.

"Not until we've worked on it, no, of course not."

"And it's right next to where?" Innocent little me. "Chick?"

"Directly across the street," Buddy smiles happily.

"And right across from Irene, too, I imagine."

"Yeah," Buddy says happily and then he sees my face. "Oh, cut it out," he says, scraping back in his chair and getting up. "This is just too much now." He stands there trembling with his hands on the back of the chair. I have never seen him like this. He almost looks like a man. "This is an opportunity, Virginia. I can't pass it up. This is where I come from. We'll have a decent place to live. We'll have a real head start. I thought you'd be pleased. It's security."

"You expect me to be happy about this? You're going to bury me in this horrible place where we'd be living right across from your girlfriend and you expect me to be happy? Do you think I'm crazy?" And I pushed past him and went into the bedroom and slammed the door.

"Well, what do you want me to do then?" yells Buddy. "Just what the hell do you want me to do?" And he goes out the door.

And all I can think of is I don't know. I don't know I don't know I don't know.

So I locked the door and I went right to Buddy's closet where all his old things are from before we got married. It was so wrong. I knew it, I don't even know what I expected to find there. A rotting corpse that would croak out some terrible secret? I was scared and excited at the same time. I found two footballs and an old pair of cleats. I found a hockey stick taped together with black tape and Buddy's name on it written in black paint. I found a box of old tennis balls none of which bounced anymore. A dog's collar with the name "Lefty." Magazines and a bunch of Hardy Boy mystery stories. In the back a bunch of folded curtains. I took everything out and nearly sneezed to death on dust. Then in the back, I found a shoebox full of photographs. Buddy on the football team. Buddy with his arms around a dog. The dog carrying a stick. Dot hanging sheets on the line grinning at whoever took the photo which was probably Buddy. Underneath everything was an envelope Scotch-taped shut but of course I opened it and inside was a photograph of a very young looking Buddy and a very young looking Irene and Irene was pregnant. I had to sit down on the bed and put my head between my knees to keep from fainting. They looked so dumb and so happy. I looked at the picture again and again. I stared a hole in it. This was the secret, this was the answer to everything in the world.

When I came out Buddy was gone. It was almost eleven-thirty when he came home. He smelled of cigarettes and beer and I knew he'd been to Townie's. When he came into the bedroom I flipped on the light. This startled him as he was used to me being asleep at this hour of the night.

"So," I said.

"What?" Buddy looked at me squinting, his hand shading his eyes as if I had the high beams on.

"I found a picture."

"What?"

"I found a picture, Buddy. You can't lie to me anymore." Of course he had never lied to me. He just hadn't told me. "I hate you," I said, starting to tremble and my eyes began to water again. "Go away." But he didn't move. He just held out his hand for the picture I was holding in mine. "I don't hate you," I said. "I don't mean that. I'm sorry I said that." I handed him the picture. He looked at it for almost a whole minute without saying a word.

"Where did you find this?" He didn't sound angry. It was as if he couldn't believe I had actually gone poking through his private things.

"In your closet."

"This isn't about you, Virginia. This isn't your life." And he dragged his eyes off the picture and looked at me.

"If Madeline has a sister or a brother it is so about my life." But I felt guilty, and I knew I was wrong. I could hardly speak, as if my throat were closing. Buddy slid the picture into his shirt pocket without looking at it again. Buddy with his arm around Irene, both of them smiling at the camera. They look so goofy and happy. Buddy had a bandana around his head and Irene was pointing her finger at the camera. Probably at Chick. No doubt he snapped the picture.

Buddy sat down on the bed. "She only lived one day."

"What?"

"The baby was born with a hole in her heart. She only lived part of one day."

"Oh no," I said. "I'm so sorry."

"She wasn't even going to keep the baby." He looked over at me as if I were a regular friend. He seemed so earnest. "She was going to give it up for adoption. We were sixteen."

"I'm really sorry."

"Irene took it hard," said Buddy. "She went away after." Buddy was still sitting on the bed and he put his head in his hands. I was standing by the bureau. Maddie was asleep in her crib, believe it or not. She can sleep through anything.

I went over and started patting her little back. I wanted her to wake up so I could hold her in my arms.

"So that's when you broke up?"

Buddy nodded. "I didn't understand. She didn't want to talk to me."

"Then I came along," I said. "And then Madeline."

Buddy shook his head. "Craziest thing."

"Well, I'm glad I had this baby," I said. "That's all I know."

Buddy didn't say anything. I guess he couldn't think of anything to say. He still had his head in his hands and I walked over and patted his shoulder and that was that. Now we act so unbelievably polite to each other. It is as if we are in a play and we have finally memorized our lines.

When I was pregnant I used to study pictures of pregnant women in *The Family of Man*. I even arranged myself in doorways like the one on page 21, one hand on my big stomach, gazing into the who-knows-what. I wanted to look like that, dreamy and happy and self-possessed. I spent my whole nine months imitating photographs in *The Family of Man*.

This morning there is a bee in the kitchen which worries me. I don't want to kill it. It is just hard to convince it to go out the door and then it bumbles off into the living room and I forget about it. In fact I am just soft-boiling an egg for Maddie's breakfast when Irene's truck pulls into the driveway and Irene hops out. I don't know if Buddy told her I know. When she comes to the door I see she has cut her hair short and dyed it red. God. I open the door with my foot. "Hi. Come on in. Don't mind the mess. Your hair looks really good like that," I tell her, thinking I am looking at a girl who has experienced tragedy in her life. It is amazing how natural I sound. "Want a glass of ice water?" I am not going to bring up the terrible sad subject unless Irene does first. What is so strange is how calm I am since I know. It was worse before, imagining. Now that I know at least I know. It is more contained that way. Otherwise, it is the entire universe that bothers you.

"Nothing, no thanks, Virginia."

"Really, your hair looks so good like that," I repeat, the soft-boiled egg in my hand now, cooling under the cold water and almost ready to tap.

"Needed a change in a big way," she says, running her hands through it. She seems out of breath. "Hey, Madeline," she says and ruffles the baby's hair. Now I am buttering a piece of toast to crumble into the egg.

"This is Maddie's favorite breakfast. She doesn't mind how slippery the egg white feels."

Irene dips a spoon in the sugar and turns it over and over watching the sugar fall back in the bowl. Then she runs her hand through her hair again as if it were falling in her eyes which it is not. "You know me and Buddy go back a ways." I nod but I don't interrupt her. "We've never really talked about it. Truthfully, Virginia, I was upset when you two got married. I guess I thought that would be me walking down the aisle with Buddy some day. So I couldn't help hating you at first. Before I met you, of course. You can understand that, can't you? I felt like my life was stolen out from under me."

"Of course I can," I say, putting a tea bag in a cup, pouring the water. God. I want to say, "Why don't you just take him, I don't want him and he loves you," but I can't because I mean it and I can't because I don't mean it. Everywhere I turn there's a stinger in me.

"But then I met you and I saw you were just a nice girl, so then I got mad at Buddy. But how can I be mad at Buddy? He did the right thing. And of course he feels so much for you and the baby." Irene cleared her throat. "So I guess all I'm saying is no hard feelings. And good luck to you. Me and Chick are thinking about moving. We've got family in California. Chick does, anyway. Next thing you know, maybe we'll be sending you postcards of the Golden Gate." This is a big piece of news. I get homesick when I think of them in California, I don't know why.

"Well," I say, "you better tell Buddy. He's planning to move in right across the street from you."

"You're kidding." Irene has no makeup on her eyes whatsoever today and as usual she does look considerably better without it.

"Right across the street. He wants to fix it up."

"I don't believe it," she says. "That old wreck?" She is half smiling.

"That's what I said too."

"Not that he couldn't fix it up nice."

"No, I know. I know he could. I just can't picture it yet. And Buddy still has one more year of school." I am looking at Irene, wondering if she knows I know, when Maddie lets out a terrible scream and then another, her whole face is clenched like a little pink fist. At first I don't know what's wrong and I think, Oh my God, but then I see that the bee is crawling around on the high chair tray and Maddie is rubbing her left arm and taking a breath for another scream. "The damn bee stung her," I say, snatching Maddie out of the chair while Irene goes after it with a magazine. Fortunately I know exactly what to do in this circumstance which is to make a poultice out of mud, and Maddie is so interested in this procedure that she stops screaming. We squat down in the flowerbed with the hose and I smear mud on her arm and then Irene brings out a pink washcloth wrapped around a couple of ice cubes and we sit there on the porch steps saying, "Bad old bee, bad old bee," and stamping our feet on the steps, all of us laughing. Then I look at Irene and she is crying. I have never imagined Irene crying, it is terrible to see she does not make a sound. Her mouth is a big O and no sound comes out at all. She shakes and shakes.

"Oh, dear," I say and I put my arms around her and suddenly I am crying, and pretty soon Maddie is crying again too, maybe just to keep us company.

"It's okay," Irene finally manages to say. "It's okay." We don't talk about anything. She doesn't tell me why she's crying, and I don't say I know, we just finally dry our eyes and blow our noses and she leaves. That afternoon Buddy comes home early. He knows about the bee sting because Irene stopped off at Mulford's and told him. After supper he is holding Maddie and she is trying to stick pieces of bread and peanut butter in his ears.

"Did she tell you they're moving?" I ask him.

"No." He hands Maddie back to me with peanut butter in her hair. He hasn't even asked if we talked about her baby. I don't think he is even wondering.

"She told me they might be moving to California," I say. I start wiping Maddie's hands with the damp dishcloth.

"When did she say that?" he asks, running water on his hands.

"Today. When she dropped by she mentioned it."

"She's not serious," says Buddy, drying his hands. "I know her."

"Okay," I say.

$\mathcal{B}$ut the big news is Chick and Irene really are moving to California. We found out yesterday at their barbecue. We weren't sure whether to go to the barbecue but we decided it just would be better to do everything normally, to go through the motions so to speak. Now everybody knew everything and best just to behave as if nothing had happened. Buddy even seemed happy that everything was out in the open, as if now we could all live like one big family maybe. I don't know. So we had our cookout but it got cut short by how Buddy took the news.

"We're moving," said Irene just as cool as a cucumber, putting ketchup on the table.

"What?" said Buddy. He stopped in mid–hamburger flip. "You're what?" He cocked his head to one side as if hearing a ridiculous joke.

"Moving. San Francisco," said Irene, taking her time with the name as if it were some delicious smooth candy in her mouth. "San Francisco, California."

"Tell me another," said Buddy. "Sure you are." He stared straight at Irene and she stared right back at him. "When." Buddy's voice was as flat as a pancake. There was no life in it at all.

"A week," said Irene, putting out the napkins and the mustard, laying down the forks and buns. "Big surprise, hey guys? Calls for a celebration I think, don't you? Chick's sister has a place for us already. Of course it's teeny, but beggars can't be choosers. Not that we'll be beggars," and she put her arm around Chick's waist. "Chick's got a job already." And they stood there together, Irene smiling as if she were waiting for someone with a camera.

"Reenie," said Buddy in a low voice. "Reenie." That is his old nickname for her. Then her face crumpled and she turned around and went into the house. After a second Buddy followed her and I just stood there and didn't look at Chick.

"What are they doing in there?" I said, but Chick didn't answer. "I don't want to get mad again. I just got over being mad."

"Let me show you something," said Chick, and he took a wrinkled snapshot out of his wallet. Not another picture.

"What am I looking at?" I asked. It was all gray with two little specks near the top.

"Those dots are Buddy and Irene climbing the granite rockface we camped near in California. No rope. I took the picture," said Chick. "I was never one for heights and somebody had to be there to pick up the pieces if they fell. That's how I always looked at it."

"What does that have to do with Buddy?" I said. "That has to do with you, Chick. I'm not particularly mad at you."

"Not particularly?" He grinned outright. "Why am I disappointed at that?" He was suddenly smiling that terribly cute smile which I now believe he knows how to turn on and off.

"I can't believe you can smile about this, Chick," I say. "And he may be your friend but he's hell to be married to. But then so am I."

"Are you?" asked Chick.

"What."

"Hell to be married to?"

"I just said so, didn't I?" I looked up at the house and saw no signs of anyone coming out anytime soon so I plopped down on the bench by the picnic table. "I know all about everything. That their baby died. I don't know what to do."

"Nothing to do," said Chick. "It was a bad time for everybody. No doubt about it. But you got to do what you can with the rest of the deck. Irene thinks she's got to leave. They need to talk about it. Now's as good a time as any, I guess."

"Don't you feel so left out?"

"All the time. Hey. Story of my life."

"I think I'm the cheese," I said. "I think we're both the cheeses."

"Well," says Chick with his smile again, "misery loves company."

I looked at the house again and then I took a bun out of a pile on the plate.

"So what are you going to do out there?" I took a big bite out of the bun.

"Run a hardware store. My brother-in-law wants a year off. Crazy sailor wants to sail around the world before he gets old."

"Really? I love hardware stores. I love all the little drawers full of nails and things. And also the way they smell."

"Well, that makes one of us," said Chick. "But the California part sounds nice."

"Oh, I know, I know," I said, as if I had spent my life there. "Good old California." Where I have never set foot. "California, here I come," I started singing. I know all the words to it.

Buddy came out of the house taking the porch steps two at a time. He was as white as a ghost. "She means it," he said to Chick. "She means it. Why? Why would you leave? Here I am about to plunk down ten grand for the dump across the street, thinking, hey, we'll be neighbors and next thing I know you're out of here. I don't get it, Chick. What's going on?"

Chick didn't seem to get it either. "Women," he said, shaking his head.

Buddy stared hard at Chick, who didn't say anything else. Then he pulled his napkin out of his belt and dropped it on the table. "I'm out of here. You ready, Virginia?"

"Well, no," I began, starting to take another bite of my bun but he grabbed my arm.

"We're going home. People you think are your friends drop a bombshell, I don't plan to stick around."

It wasn't a good time to argue. I felt sorry for Buddy, to tell the truth, I really did. I felt sorry for Buddy and I felt sorry for Irene. I also felt sorry for me. The only person I didn't feel sorry for was Chick. He seemed to be okay with everything. "I'm easy," said Chick. Well, the hell with him.

Irene came out of the house but she didn't watch us go. She just kept fooling around with the napkins. I waved but she didn't see me. Chick went and took a few burgers off the fire and then I didn't see any more because Buddy peeled out of there.

"Why do you think they're moving?" I asked Buddy. He shook his head.

"It's insane, Virginia," he said, very agitated. "What does she think she's going to do out there?" Fortunately this was not a question he expected me to answer. Why not? is all I could think of. Why not move if you are in love with somebody who is married to somebody else? Why stick around and have to stare at him the whole time? It made perfect sense to me.

"Do you think it upsets her to see so much of you?" I asked very tentatively.

"Why should it?" said Buddy, but he cut me a quick look.

"Why should it?" he asked again, as if he actually wanted my opinion. "We aren't doing anything wrong."

"Because she used to be in love with you, I guess, and vice versa. Maybe there's some of it left."

"That's ridiculous," he said, but he didn't say anything else.

When we got home he just went into the bedroom and lay down across the bed. "I'm beat, Virginia," he said. "Gonna catch a few z's."

I went over to Dot's above the garage where she had Maddie, who was still up. I told her we came back unexpectedly early. I told her Irene and Chick were moving to California. "I know about the baby that died," I said. Might as well get everything all over with.

Dot nodded, looking at me uncertainly. "She was sixteen. I told her I'd raise the baby for her but she had her own ideas."

"Well, this is my baby girl," I said, picking Maddie up from Dot's lap. I don't feel as mean as I sound. I'm just very definite. Dot got up and started to follow me and Maddie down the stairs. "I just want to be by myself, Dot, if you don't mind." So Dot stayed put. I'll say this for her. She knows when to let a person alone.

I cleaned out the icebox because we will be going back to Pittsburgh and Dot will have the house for herself again. In the way back of the freezer I unwrap the tinfoil that I am sure is a piece of our wedding cake but it turns out to be pizza. So then I have to find it, just to find it. I unwrap everything in there and none of it is wedding cake. I guess it got thrown out by mistake long ago.

Chick and Irene are supposed to leave the day after tomorrow and Buddy and I are just moping around for our separate reasons which we don't want to talk about. We are being nice and polite to each other. It's all we can do. We don't even have anything to fight about, not really. I guess we are both thinking we can act nice to each other for the rest of our lives and just stay together for the baby's sake. We don't have to fight. We just act nice and try not to feel anything, that's what I've got in mind. How can you be mad at someone who never loved you in the first place? It was all just a big accident. Buddy is trying his hardest now. And me too. And as long as we're stuck with each other, we might as well go to the fair, that's the way I look at it. It's something to do and I think Madeline will like the colored lights and the way the Ferris wheel looks in the dark. When we get there I take Maddie on the merry-go-round and she hangs on to the horse very seriously while I stand next to her, I think she believes it is a real horse from the way she gently pats its ears and lays her face against its dark hard mane. By the time we get off

Buddy has disappeared into the crowd. I thought he would wait for us.

I pick Maddie up and start wandering around, half looking for Buddy, half just looking around at everybody. There are lots of people here and they are all having a good time. The music is that carny music. Nothing you can dance to, and a sort of polka at one end of the fairgrounds and somebody has lost a puppy which keeps running around through my legs. Maddie and I walk around and then I spy Chick, of all people, and he is looking at me, waiting for me to see him. He stands next to the booth for the Ferris wheel and he taps his watch impatiently as if he were waiting for me. Smiling. This makes me feel sadder than anything, actually.

"Hey," I say, and I feel so miserable but I'm so used to feeling miserable that by now it's like a little companion.

"Bad day?" he says. "Cheer up. Life goes on. You're at the fair. You're supposed to look happy. Here, let me buy the little lady and her mama a cotton candy." Well, cotton candy is my favorite thing in all the world, I am sorry to say, so I say thank you and then we let Maddie have little shreds of it to put in her mouth and pretty soon her face is pink and her tongue is pink and all three of us are sticky and Chick is saying, "Take a look at this," which is a small bear in a red hat and a man trying to make it dance to his horrible accordion. God.

"That's pitiful," I say, and Chick says, "Well, you're right, I guess," and we move away over to where they are throwing balls at ducks.

"That's how I met Buddy," I say to Chick. "He hit a million of those and gave me all his teddy bears." So Chick picks up a few balls and hits a million ducks and hands me the fake gold bracelet that he wins. "Oh," I say, "I can't really accept this, Chick, thanks anyway."

"Virginia," says Chick, smiling his nice smile full of parentheses, and sliding it on my wrist, "you've got to lighten up."

"I don't know where Buddy went," I say after a while and it turns out Chick doesn't know where Irene got to either but neither of us is looking very hard as we are too busy with Maddie, who is excited and wants to get down and run around which is impossible here. It is just too crowded. Chick takes Maddie up the wide silver slide and I walk over to the edge of the fairgrounds and I spy the puppy shivering by some bushes in the woods and I am tiptoeing toward him when I hear voices and then people crying. And as I get closer who do I see? I see Buddy and Irene, and they are hanging on to each other for dear life, and Buddy's shoulders are shaking and Irene has just buried her face in his neck. Crying their damn eyes out together. It is much worse than if I'd found them naked. I walk away as quietly as I can but they wouldn't hear me if I screamed in their ears.

I feel so extremely calm when I come back. "Hey, Chick," I say, "could you give me a lift home? I'm so tired all of a sudden and I just really need to get home. I'm sure Buddy will understand."

Chick doesn't ask me any searching questions. "Sure," he says, "anything to oblige," and he drops me and Maddie at the house. He doesn't even say good-bye, he just tips his imaginary hat and I climb out with the baby.

Nobody is home, of course. The house is quiet. I can hear the sounds of the fair though, since this is a small town, and you can hear the barker and the fireworks and all the other stuff that goes along with it. I wonder who will win the car. I am packing, of course. I pack my things and Maddie's. Maddie plays on the floor by my feet. I get one suitcase packed and then another. I put a lot of diapers in a big duffel bag. I pack a couple of my books and then I pack some food. I don't know where I am going, but I certainly can't stay another second. I pack sheets and towels and my toothbrush. I pack my shampoo and Maddie's powder. I am a packing fool. Maddie sits calmly on the floor playing with the set of measuring cups.

Then I'm not sure what to do so I drag everything into the kitchen. I pick Maddie up and I sit on top of our bags like an idiot queen. Where am I going? Nowhere. Where do I have to go? Nowhere. So there I am without the slightest idea what to do next when a butter knife falls off the table of its own free will. Swear to God, I didn't touch it, and pretty soon I hear tires coming up the driveway, then a door slams and I hear footsteps on the porch. *Knock knock.*

"You ready, Virginia?" It is Chick's voice.

"Oh, hi," I say, "it's you."